Telescope

A Story Cycle

Essential Prose Series 171

Canada Council **Conseil des Arts**
for the Arts **du Canada**

ONTARIO ARTS COUNCIL
CONSEIL DES ARTS DE L'ONTARIO

an Ontario government agency
un organisme du gouvernement de l'Ontario

Canadä

Guernica Editions Inc. acknowledges the support of the Canada Council
for the Arts and the Ontario Arts Council. The Ontario Arts Council
is an agency of the Government of Ontario.

We acknowledge the financial support of the Government of Canada.

Telescope

A Story Cycle

Allan Weiss

**GUERNICA
EDITIONS**
TORONTO • BUFFALO • LANCASTER (U.K.)
2019

Michael Mirolla, editor
David Moratto, Interior and cover design
Guernica Editions Inc.
1569 Heritage Way, Oakville, (ON), Canada L6M 2Z7
2250 Military Road, Tonawanda, N.Y. 14150-6000 U.S.A.
www.guernicaeditions.com

Distributors:
University of Toronto Press Distribution,
5201 Dufferin Street, Toronto (ON), Canada M3H 5T8
Gazelle Book Services, White Cross Mills
High Town, Lancaster LA1 4XS U.K.

First edition.
Printed in Canada.

Legal Deposit—Third Quarter
Library of Congress Catalog Card Number: 2019930488
Library and Archives Canada Cataloguing in Publication
Title: Telescope : a story cycle / Allan Weiss.
Names: Weiss, Allan 1956- author.
Series: Essential prose series ; 171.
Description: First edition. | Series statement: Essential
prose series ; 171 | Short stories.
Identifiers: Canadiana (print) 20190050225 |
Canadiana (ebook) 20190050241 | ISBN 9781771834285 (softcover) |
ISBN 9781771834292 (EPUB) | ISBN 9781771834308 (Kindle)
Classification: LCC PS8595.E4886 T45 2019 | DDC C813/.6—dc23

Contents

Moving Day

I N 1968 MY family moved to Ville St. Laurent. After years
of promises and declarations, my father finally bought
a house, and we prepared to move on May 1. That was
Moving Day in Montreal, where one day has always been
set aside for leases to end. That may have been one of the
many rules about renting that my Dad wanted to escape—
along with not making too much noise, and not running a
business at home that might get the landlord in trouble and
our family evicted.

Dad announced his decision at dinner one day in early
January. My sister and I had just returned to school after the
Christmas break, and we were finally getting back into our
routines, and together again with our friends.

"It's official," he said. "We're going to find a house of our
own at last."

My sister looked horrified. "I don't want to move!" she
said. "I like it here. All my friends are here."

"You'll make new ones."

"It'll be better for us in the long run," my mother said, stirring her goulash with a fork to cool it off.

Their answers were like lines out of a TV show, and I half-seriously wondered if my parents had rehearsed this whole scene beforehand. I was really torn about it. Naturally, I didn't want to leave my friends, my school, and my neighbourhood, either. Howard Cohen was my best friend that year, and we were the leaders of a small "alliance" that vowed we would protect each other if Steve Thornton, the school bully, attacked any of us. I knew the teachers at Bedford School—which ones were "strict," which ones nice, if not from experience then from what others said. I didn't want to give up the kids, the streets, the back yards, and the stores I knew.

But a house meant my own room at last, as my father had long promised. It meant I could have friends come over to play football in my back yard without Mrs. Selinsky, the landlady, shooing them away if we tore up the grass too much. And a house meant something different and exciting, a space beyond what was old and boring. I figured I could get used to it.

"I don't want to move," my sister repeated, then crossed her arms and fell silent, eyes lowered to her plate. My father went on about how he'd finally have a place of his own to set up his bookkeeping business, how we'd be in a quiet neighbourhood (I didn't know what he was talking about; Goyer wasn't noisy), how we'd never throw money away on rent again.

"Do we have to change schools in the middle of the year?" I asked. "Couldn't we keep going to Bedford till the end?"

"No. How would you do that?"

My sister was just finishing Grade Seven, and would be in high school next year anyway; that would mean two new schools in one year. It made no sense for either of us to change schools with only a month and a half to go.

"It'll be all right," my mother said, again as if she were following the TV script. But I knew better.

* * *

So much happened in the world that spring that our move sometimes faded completely from my mind. My father watched *Pulse News* on CFCF every night before supper, and it became impossible to escape the scary, violent stories that Andrew Marquis reported. I was fully aware that the United States and the Soviet Union could start World War III any time, over anything, but that was a hazy fear, a what-if that meant little more than the basis for some of the science-fiction movies my father and I watched on Saturday afternoons. What we saw on the news, though, couldn't be pushed away: American reporters were reporting from Vietnam, with film of wounded, wide-eyed soldiers being carried on stretchers, especially after the Tet Offensive.

Usually my father made some kind of comment when he watched the news, but now he would sit wordlessly, with his hands folded between his knees, a sick and angry look on his face as if what was going on was a personal attack. He hated the Russians for what they'd done to Hungary and the other countries in Eastern Europe. He saw them doing the same thing to people so far away they might as well have been on another planet—but we could watch, now, and see jumpy but clear pictures of the jungles and helicopters, and men looking over their shoulders at the camera.

"Turn that off," my mother said one time, though her eyes were riveted on the screen. "We've seen enough."

"Shh," my father said, gently.

"I wish we had a colour TV," I said, for what must have been the hundredth time. I both wanted, and didn't want, to stop watching, too.

"We can't afford one," my father said. "Yet."

After the international news, my father pushed himself out of the living-room armchair with a grunt. He was starting to gain weight then. He would drive all over Montreal delivering or picking up ledgers, and often had lunch at delis near his clients' businesses, on St. Lawrence and Ste. Catherine. At first, he brought home grease-stained paper bags with leftovers, then decided it wasn't worth the bother.

"Goddamn Commies," he said. "Everywhere they go there's nothing but trouble."

I agreed, and I dreamed of someday doing something spectacular to the world's Communists—slaughtering them by the thousands. There had to be a way to get rid of them, without killing everybody else at the same time, and one day we'd figure out how. They were bullies, violent people with minds we could never fathom.

* * *

In March, my father told us he'd found a house in Ville St. Laurent, where prices were lower and a good number of Jewish people lived. He had us all meet in the living room, where we sat on the plastic-covered chesterfield and gazed at the photo from the real-estate agent. The house looked tiny and squat compared to our duplex. How would we all fit in it?

"It's a good bungalow, not too old, and it's got a big basement I can use for the office. And a nice back yard." He looked at me. "You'll like that."

Sheila had only glanced at the photo; now she refused to look up from her shoes.

"And like I said," my father continued, his voice cheery as he tried to pretend we were thrilled with the show he was putting on, "you'll finally have your own rooms like you're supposed to."

"You're too old to share now," my mother said.

I knew she was right. But this was starting to get serious; I began to believe it would really happen.

"So?" Sheila said, without much energy. She wanted her own room as much as I did.

As moving day came nearer, the house—as we called our duplex flat, even if it wasn't a house—began to look and even sound stranger. The rooms were usually crowded with stuff: toys and school supplies in the room Sheila and I shared; files, ledgers, and the bulky electric adding machine in my father's office; papers and books everywhere else. My father's paint-by-numbers pictures hung over the chesterfield and my parents' bed. But now dishes, books, and magazines began disappearing into cardboard boxes that my mother brought home from Steinberg's. Opening or closing a light meant leaning over stacks of cartons printed with the logos of cereals and brands of spaghetti we never bought. Rooms developed bizarre new echoes.

At school I told my friends I was moving soon, that we

were buying a house and wouldn't have to throw our money away to a landlord any more. Howard gave me a sharp look. I thought it was because he and his family were too poor to buy a house, and I felt bad for him. My mother had told me recently that Howard's father had a bad back and couldn't work; his mother did dressmaking to bring in some money, but not a lot.

"You're really going?" Howard asked.

"Yeah." I didn't know what else to say. Kenny Wasserman, a kid I was sometimes friends, sometimes enemies with, was part of our alliance now and looked on wonderingly. I saw him absently scratching his cheek. Jeffrey Gold, one of the quietest kids I ever knew, was too busy counting his hockey cards to pay much attention. I'd be leaving them all, without any say in the matter. It wasn't fair.

So I confronted my father at supper. "Do I have to change Hebrew Schools, too?"

"Eh?" He obviously hadn't thought about it. From his frustrated expression it was clear I'd won. "Fine! You'll go to the old Hebrew School." We made our plans: He'd drive me to and from Beth Hamedrash shul on Tuesdays and Thursdays.

* * *

A few weeks before we moved, we were all sitting in the living room watching *Daniel Boone* when the show stopped suddenly and a sign came up: "Special News Bulletin."

"We interrupt this program for a special new bulletin," the announcer said, as if he needed to tell us, and I sat there frightened and thrilled. It was something horrible, something exciting, and the first thought that went through my mind was those tests of the emergency broadcasting system, with the loud *beeeep*. Was there an attack? "From NBC News, here is David Brinkley reporting." My father leaned forward, and I could tell he was scared, too. My mother watched with her brows knit, eyes wide.

Then came the story. "Dr. Martin Luther King has been shot." I barely knew who he was — he was the leader of the American Negroes, or some of them. I couldn't tell if he was one of the leaders who caused the riots. The news was full of riots and Vietnam protests; the Americans seemed to be going crazy. I waited for a reaction from my parents, but they didn't seem to know what to think, either. The news wasn't as bad as we'd feared, but it wasn't good. Brinkley told us about how King had been brought to a hospital, how the police were looking for a suspect. There were scenes of Negro women crying.

"Who's he?" my sister asked. I was thankful it was Sheila who asked first. I didn't want to look dumb.

"A good man," my father said. "One of the good ones."

But there were scenes of marches he'd led. He'd caused trouble, stirred things up. It wasn't a good idea to do that, because you never knew how others might react. It was better to stay quiet.

For a while, the Vietnam War wasn't the first story each night; everything seemed to centre on Martin Luther King's death, and the huge funeral in Atlanta.

"This is a very moving day for America," one of the announcers said, and it reminded me that I had my own things to worry about.

* * *

I saw our new house only once before we moved in, just before May 1. The place smelled of fresh paint. All I could see were big, empty rooms, including a living room with bare wood floors that creaked, and a kitchen missing its fridge and stove. With no curtains on the windows, the house glared with sunlight casting odd, pale shadows. I felt as if we were being watched by all the houses around us. Between what was going to be my bedroom and Sheila's was the door to the basement; I opened it carefully to keep from smearing the paint, walked partway down the stairs, and saw a vast expanse of checkered linoleum.

I kept expecting my sister to say that she hated it, but she took my mother's guided tour silently. I was glad of that— I couldn't have tolerated her whining today.

"Look at the back yard," my mother said to us. She opened the rear door at the far end of the kitchen, holding it so we could see through to the square of lawn beyond. At our duplex we had access not only to our own back yard (at least, when Mrs. Selinsky wasn't complaining), but the ones on either side as well. Here, the lawn was fully enclosed by bushes on the sides and a solid wooden fence at the back. A large tree stood in the far corner.

"It's all ours," my mother said. "No landlady."

I was about to say that it was smaller than our old one, but refrained. She probably knew it.

* * *

May 1 was a school day, but my parents didn't make us attend either school. We watched the movers—a couple of huge French guys smelling of cigarette smoke—haul boxes out to the Allied Van Lines truck. My father drove my sister and me to our grandmother's apartment so we wouldn't get in the way; Bubby let us watch TV all day, except for when she served us scrambled eggs and Niblets.

At 4:30 Dad came to pick us up. He looked tired and not terribly happy, and I wondered if he was regretting the move as much as we were. He drove us straight to the new house, although I wished he'd taken us to the old one so I could check one last time for anything I might have forgotten. I'd gone through my room a dozen times, finding the odd Lego brick or soldier in corners or under the radiator, but I was convinced that things I'd lost over the years were just waiting for me if only I looked long enough.

The house looked different with all its boxes, and with the new, suffocating gold carpet covering the living room floor. We still had no curtains, so my mother had put up old sheets in the meantime. The house still smelled of paint, as well as the chemical odour of the gold-streaked linoleum in the hall. My own room was crowded with boxes; the dresser I'd had to share with my sister (she was getting a new one of her own) and my bed stood crookedly in its centre. I started shifting things around to make space for myself. At least now I wouldn't have to answer to my sister for my every move, for where every object might end up.

"*Oy*, what a mess," my mother said as she examined the rooms. "Start fixing it all up. Put your stuff away."

From the things she said I gathered she and my father had spent the move ordering the men about, arguing with them about how many boxes there ought to be. "One of them is missing, I know it," she said.

"What's in it?" my father asked. He wanted to go down into the basement and set up his office.

"Towels and plates. They must have lost them." She

looked through some of the now-unsealed boxes. "Sugar," she muttered.

At that moment, a low rumble outside grew into a roar. I turned in time to see an airplane, flying shockingly low, zip across the little window in our front door. We were right on the flight routes into Dorval Airport.

I managed to get most of my clothes and toys unpacked that evening—just enough to make my room look familiar. After supper, we watched TV in our new living room; I lay on the springy carpet and kept getting distracted by the lights of the cars against the "curtains." I'd never lived at street level before. Meanwhile, passing airplanes drowned out the shows at critical points.

I knew that I'd never get used to this—and I shouldn't have to. Moving hadn't been *my* idea.

I couldn't sleep that night, or at least not until past midnight. I could tell the time because I heard the end of the late *Pulse News* playing low but audibly in the living room. The reports were focusing on Vietnam again; the riots that followed King's shooting were over, although other ones, for different reasons—mostly the war—kept breaking out. France seemed to be having a revolution. The Czechoslovakians were trying to be less Communist. I heard my father close the TV set, then pass my slightly open door on the way to his and my mother's room, whispering something to himself.

I couldn't stop thinking about what would happen at my new school the next day, how I'd cope with a new teacher and a classroom full of strangers. My mother repeated over and over that I'd make new friends, as if you just went up to some kid you'd never seen before and suddenly became friends. At least Hebrew School followed immediately afterward; once regular school let out, I could head to the shul on Mackenzie and see my real friends. I fell asleep while a plane passed by.

* * *

The next morning my mother walked me down to the school. I didn't want her to take me any further than the steel-mesh fence, but she came inside. Gardenview looked all right—I'd been picturing a school out of a nineteenth-century British novel, with high walls and narrow windows. My mother brought me to the office, where a secretary in a curly hairdo took over to lead me to my class. By the time I turned around to wave goodbye to my mother she was on her way out the door. I knew she had a busy day ahead fixing up the new house, but she could have stayed long enough to say more than "Okay" to everything the secretary said. I half-wanted to see the new class, half-dreaded it. How different would St. Laurent be? What were the rules? I was wearing the new sweater my mother had bought me for the occasion; where was I supposed to hang it?

Room 6 was down a side corridor, and was identified by a triangular piece of black metal above the open door, with the "6" in white. That was the opposite of Bedford School, which had black on white, but otherwise, from a first glance, it seemed the classroom was pretty much the same as Bedford's. All the kids looked at me as the secretary led me inside.

"Miss Acker," she said to the teacher. "Here is your new student, Lawrence Teitel."

Miss Acker was a tall woman with thick glasses and a stiff smile. I recognized that smile from some of my hockey cards—all curved lips, no teeth showing, no shine in the eyes. "Welcome, Lawrence."

"Hi."

"There's a seat back there for you." I hunted past the strangers' faces and found it. The desks and chairs in the room were the same blond, glossy wood I was familiar with; the desks even had the strange round inkwell hole that no longer served its original purpose. The Protestant School Board of Greater Montreal calendar, with its blue numbers for school days and red ones for holidays, hung on the cupboard door. Even the round electric clock looked the same. As I sat down, scraping the chair loudly, I heard snickers behind me. Two girls giggled to each other beside me.

"We're doing arithmetic, Lawrence," Miss Acker said. I wished she would stop talking to me. "Did you do fractions at your old school?"

"Yeah."

"Common denominators?"

"Yeah." My mouth started to go dry.

"Good. We'll see how you do." I was afraid she was going to ask me to get up in front of the class and show off what I knew, but she turned her attention to the blackboard instead.

"Your *old* school," somebody whispered. For some reason, he thought it was funny. Then I realized I was still wearing my sweater, and didn't know what to do with it.

I stayed out of sight most of the morning. I was amazed at the kids' behaviour; Miss Acker didn't know how to control a class, or they were just uncontrollable. At recess we filed out to the schoolyard, and one of the kids took the trouble to say, "Nice sweater" in a richly sarcastic voice. I didn't know who he was or why he felt it necessary to say that, but I vowed never to wear it again.

I went home for lunch. I'd gotten used to the paint smell overnight, but noticed it again as soon as I entered. I ate my peanut butter sandwich silently, watching my mother rush in and out of the kitchen. She was still struggling to organize things, especially with the new fridge and stove standing in awkward positions, and unpacked boxes getting in her way in the hallway and living room.

"So how's your new school?" she asked when she finally felt she could sit down opposite me.

I shrugged. There was nothing to say. Or at least there was nothing I could tell her. Luckily, my sister came in then, and so I didn't have to come up with any more answers.

After school my father drove me to the shul, and there I got back with Howard, Jeffrey, Wayne, Kenny. I told them about the school, about Miss Acker. "I don't like the kids," I said, out of loyalty to them and because it was the truth.

"Are they Jewish?" Wayne asked, as if that mattered.

"Yeah, I think so." But they were still alien; St. Laurent was like another planet. We traded a few cards, although hockey season was over and all we had were "Monkees" cards that Kenny refused to collect.

* * *

For the next couple of days, I tried to stay out of Miss Acker's line of sight. Sometimes she would ask painfully easy questions, and I'd put up my hand, hoping I could speed things along. It was like in oral reading, when the teacher would call on the worst readers, as if trying to waste all our time. Generally, though, I struggled to keep my hands folded on my desk as I'd been taught at Bedford, although no one else seemed to be doing it.

As bad as Miss Acker was, the kids were simply impossible to understand. I noticed they called each other, and me, by last names rather than first names; they used words like "fuck" and "shit" which the kids at Bedford never did, even after school. I didn't know why the kids here were so different. I kept looking for an answer, sure I could find it if I listened, just kept my mouth shut, and paid attention.

But then I made a mistake. We were doing science, and Miss Acker asked if anybody could answer her question about how many planets there were. I knew about the solar system because my father had taught me, and he'd let me read his science fiction magazines. I found myself talking about the planets longer than I planned to, mostly because she kept asking me more questions. "Which is the biggest? Which is the furthest from the sun?" I wanted her to ask the others, but she kept coming back to me. Finally, she asked me about whether there were really canals on Mars. I knew that there weren't, but I said, "I don't know," and looked down at my desk till she left me alone.

At recess the kids started in on me. "Hey, Spaceman!" "What's your spaceship like?" I tried smiling, but they just kept going. It wasn't a joke any more.

One of them came right up to me against the fence. "I asked you a question. What does Mars look like?" When I didn't answer he said: "Eh? Spaceman?" He was tall, thin, with a mouthful of braces.

"Leave me alone."

"Leave me alone."

It made no sense. I'd done nothing to them. I didn't want to be there in the first place. I tried to walk away from them but three or four stood in my way; others were playing Champ in the squares beyond, and I wanted to watch one of the games.

"Hey, Spaceman?"

When they finally got tired of waiting for an answer the kids moved away. But I knew I was marked.

After school I walked home keeping my head bowed, watching the sidewalk slide by beneath my feet. I'd known practically every crack on the sidewalks of Goyer. Here I'd have to watch every step, make sure I didn't trip over anything. But the trees were budding, and I couldn't resist looking up at them sometimes, as if they had something to offer.

* * *

The "Spaceman" business continued, day after day. It naturally led to fights. "Shut up" didn't work, and neither did turning my back. Pushing led to punches. At Bedford you could identify the bullies and stay out of their way, unless they tried to take your hockey card money or they simply felt like beating someone up. But these weren't guys you could single out; they were just the regular kids. I'd once told my mother about Steve Thornton, and she'd said: "Just ignore him and he'll stop." But I knew better, I understood life in schoolyards more than she did: Bullies didn't stop till you fought back.

One recess the tall kid with braces started up again. We ended up wrestling on the pavement, sometimes getting punches in but mostly just grabbing. A teacher came running out of the school and hauled us off the ground, then sent us inside. That was when I got sent to the principal's office for the first time in my life. The kid and I sat for twenty minutes in the school office, just outside the door with the black sign saying: "Mr. R. G. Carrington Principal." We waited for something to happen, ignoring each other as we watched the secretary scribble things on a large sheet of lined paper.

Mr. Carrington's door opened at last. He was a huge man with a thin moustache. "Come in here, you two." I thought this was my chance at last; I'd tell him what was happening to me, and he'd put a stop to it. That was his job.

Mr. Carrington sat behind his desk, which was mounded with papers; a picture of Queen Elizabeth II hung above his head. There were hard wooden chairs facing him, but he didn't tell us to sit down.

"I don't want any more fighting, all right?"

"But he started it—!" I said.

"I don't care who started it! That's not my concern." He leaned forward in his chair, making its leather squeak. "No more, is that understood? Now go back to your classes."

"But—!"

"Dismissed."

So that was it. I was shocked but not really surprised.

The one thing I knew I couldn't do was tell my parents, Miss Acker, or anyone else. That would be the end of me. I had to fight my own battles—that was obvious, not just from what my father had always said but also from what I knew. You couldn't be a cry-baby. Visions of my mother marching into the school to defend me sent chills through me.

"So how was school?" she asked me every day.

"Fine."

At last, she asked me: "Aren't you making any friends?"

"No."

"Why? How are the kids? They're all right?"

"No." But I didn't elaborate. I couldn't tell her how much I hated them. I couldn't tell her they were mean for no reason I could come up with, and I didn't think she'd believe me anyway.

"Why, what's wrong?"

"Nothing."

She waited for me to say more. "They're making trouble?"

"Never mind."

Finally, she dropped the subject.

During classes I was bored; at recess and lunch hour, before we returned to the safety of Room 6, I was terrified. I had no idea when someone would decide to launch into the teasing, or pick a fight. It was ridiculous, it was so crazy.

Sheila, meanwhile, wasn't doing much better. I saw her every now and then among the Grade 7s, always alone. At school — even back at Bedford — we always pretended that we didn't know each other, and I refused to walk home with her if my parents asked me to or if I ran into Sheila in the schoolyard after the final bell. Now, I wasn't sure which of us would suffer more if it became known, or at least too obvious, that we were related.

Not all the kids seemed anxious to pick fights, of course. I was put together with Danny Elbaum and Paul Schneider on a group project making a miniature tropical village for Geography. It was supposed to be from some island full of jungles and collections of grass huts. We got along all right, but they had their own friends. At Hebrew School I made sure my real friends knew what I was dealing with. The worst words they came up with were "jerk" and "stinker," and I was amazed at how different the two districts were. It was hard to believe I still lived in Montreal.

For the next few weeks I managed to avoid having Miss Acker notice me. I hated her for what she'd done to me, just as much as I hated the kids who continued to pick on me. She should have known better, but I'd long noticed that grownups knew nothing about our world. I had to keep her out of my life, to keep myself safe. If I kept my head down, in more ways than one, I'd be all right.

One day at lunch my mother insisted on asking me about the kids again. "Are you still having trouble with them?"

"No." That was almost true. I was having fewer fights, though I was still known as "Spaceman."

"Are you sure?"

"They're just not …" I couldn't think of a word that fit. "Nice" was ridiculous; I wanted to say "civilized."

"They're spoiled," Ma said.

That made sense. The new neighbourhood was richer than our old one; everybody lived in houses, not duplexes, and despite how much I hated St. Laurent I couldn't help seeing that the area was nicer than Goyer. More trees lined the street, and some were already blossoming. Flowers were planted in bunches across the house fronts, not just in tight little rock gardens near the stairs. Our own house was finally starting to lose its paint smell. If only the kids—

"Spoiled rotten."

I looked up at her, and saw something in her eyes. Maybe I was imagining it, but I got the sense she'd run into the same thing, that she'd tried to make friends with the neighbours and gotten nowhere. I realized that I never saw any of our neighbours come to the house, the way her friends on Goyer had done. She'd often have tea with Mrs. Cohen or Mrs. Wasserman — even when I was enemies with their sons that week.

"They're not *haymische*," she said. I didn't know what the word meant, but I felt as if I didn't have to. "They're not the same kind of people."

* * *

I counted the days till the end of school. Then, in early June, we were watching TV when that notice flashed again on the screen: "Special News Bulletin," it said, and again my heart jumped. My mother said: "*Oy*, what now?"

"We interrupt this program for a special news bulletin ..."

I stared at the screen as a reporter came on, and announced that Robert Kennedy had been shot. I didn't know very much about who he was, but I knew he was John Kennedy's brother, and I remembered being very small and learning that the President had been shot. "Our" President, I'd thought. I knew Robert Kennedy wasn't "our" anything, but that didn't matter.

"My God," my father said. "My God."

"That family," my mother said. "No *mazel*."

Robert Kennedy wasn't dead, and half my mind said that he wouldn't die; it would be too much. The other half didn't know. The TV showed tape of Robert Kennedy walking through a crowd, then the camera shook, and all you could see was him lying on the floor, his head supported by someone.

"Why'd they shoot him?" my sister asked, and I knew it was a stupid question. I think even she realized that. Nobody answered, because there was no answer. It made no sense. As the reporters came on, telling their stories, I watched silently, and so did the rest of my family. There was nothing to say.

Colour Blind

OR MY MOTHER's sixtieth birthday, I transferred our old 8mm home movies onto videotape. I sorted the small gray plastic reels by date—as far as I could determine from the way we and the cars looked. Then I spliced the films together using my father's old Kodak Home Splicer and some scotch tape; the original splicing tape had either been used up or gone missing. One of the earliest films I found showed my Dad helping my sister, who couldn't have been more than four, skate around on the rink at Beaver Lake on Mount Royal. He bent awkwardly forward in his thick black overcoat as he held my sister's mittened hands, and she seemed to love skittering around, laughing as she watched her feet refuse to stay in place. My mother must have been doing the filming for a change, and the camera was never steady.

Another reel showed me and my sister sitting opposite each other at a small table, colouring in a large sheet together.

We kept our eyes lowered, focused on our work and away from the glare of the bank of blinding lights. It always amazed me how Sheila could keep between the lines, no matter how dull the crayons, even when she didn't make a protective border near the edges first. And she filled in the spaces evenly, so that the colours became magically solid and full; she left no white strips the way I did, and whatever she coloured seemed to float off the page, the way red chalk shimmered against our Grade 1 blackboard. She could tell the difference between the greens and browns, between the blues and purples, without having to look at the paper wrappers; I didn't understand why it was so much harder for me, and figured it must be because she had better eyes, somehow, even though she wore glasses. In the film, we couldn't have been more than seven and five years old, but by then she already knew how to do things I knew I'd never learn.

* * *

When we moved to Ville St. Laurent, the change was tough for me but terrible for Sheila. Like me, she didn't want to leave behind her friends, her school, everything she was used to. But at least I didn't completely reject my Dad's arguments: that we'd have a house of our own, not a place we rented; that the new neighbourhood was "better," meaning richer; that, most of all, we'd both finally get our own rooms. Just the thought of no longer having to share a room with her could make me forget, if only for a moment, about my losses. But Sheila just rolled her eyes in frustration and said: "I don't *care!*" even though she really did.

She had as much trouble as I did making friends at Gardenview, without the excuse of being picked on and even jumped from behind in the schoolyard. There were girl bullies, too, I knew; I heard reports from other kids about them, and found the idea incredible. But fat Lisa Feinstein never seemed to go anywhere near my sister. Still, Sheila was perpetually angry or miserable, and she'd even sometimes make faces at the window when an airplane flew by on its way to or from Dorval Airport, as if they and their noise were the problem.

Every day after school she'd complain to my mother, or save it up for supper so she could tell my father when he came upstairs from the office in the basement.

"I hate it here!" "Mrs. Goldfarb is mean. Why can't I go back? At least Miss Adamski was nice." "It wasn't *my* idea to move!"

"Look," my father said to her one time, "you're going to have to get used to it, okay? We're here, and that's final."

One way Sheila held onto Bedford School was by refusing to change how she dressed for school. She kept wearing her tunic, even though most of the girls at Gardenview didn't. Gardenview had a dress code, but no requirement like the one at Bedford that girls wear black or navy blue tunics and white blouses. The other girls would wear dresses or skirts, with stockings that often bagged around the knees. Yet every day Sheila put on her old tunic and leotards, as if she was begging to be teased, trying to make it harder to make friends.

One afternoon just before supper I passed her room and saw her sitting at her desk, arms crossed. She hadn't changed out of her tunic yet, and she just stared at something — her homework, I supposed—with her jaw tightly set. On a shelf above the desk, her collection of Barbie and Skipper dolls stood in an even row on their rod stands, as carefully lined up as my soldiers were when I had a battle. For some reason I couldn't take my eyes off her as she gazed downward. Suddenly she noticed me. "*What?*" she demanded.

I had no answer. I wasn't sure what I was doing there. She looked fragile and wounded, like an accident victim.

She rolled her eyes, sighed furiously, and got up just enough to reach over and slam the door in my face.

"Hey!" my father shouted from downstairs. I heard him stomp up the basement stairs. "What the hell is going *on!*" I ran into my own room and closed my door quietly. "I've had enough of this!" I knew he was standing outside my sister's door. "I'm tired of your attitude! Tired of listening to you!" I sat on my bed, listening with satisfaction as he told her off. "We're not going back so you'd better just get used to it. Eh?"

The worst thing for Sheila was giving up her after-school skating. She would walk over to Neighbourhood House on Darlington, where she'd catch a school bus to an arena on Jean Talon for lessons and to be part of shows. We'd sometimes go to see her perform with the club. The girls (and a few boys) danced and spun to classical music or songs from movies like *The Sound of Music* and *Fiddler on the Roof.* Sheila often practised at the rink in Kent Park with the other girls, doing spins and figure-eights. I could never get as comfortable on hockey skates as she was in her white figure skates. And I found myself shamefully envying how smooth, how right she seemed when she was on the ice. She once tried to show me how to lift one foot high off the ice and curl around on the other, but I kept falling till I finally stomped off to sit on the hardened mound of snow beside the rink. I didn't want to be a figure skater, I told myself, so what was the big deal? I was seven or eight, and still thought I might someday play for the Canadiens, so it didn't matter that I couldn't skate like a girl.

Now, we lived far from Neighbourhood House, and Dad wasn't prepared to drive her around, too. The best he could do was sign her up for the summer skating school at the St. Laurent Community Centre on Decarie.

I held my peace and sympathized, at least at the beginning. I wanted things to go better for her, I wanted her to make the whole move easier by not adding to my sense that it had been a terrible mistake. But all she did was keep confirming that I was right. What my Dad told her was true: There was nothing she or I could do about being there; we were stuck. So if things were really as bad as I thought they were, I was in serious trouble.

It's hard for both of us! I yelled at her, silently. *Not just you!*

Actually, in some ways it was easier for me because I could still see my friends in Hebrew School. I still had another year to go before my Bar Mitzvah, and I was determined to keep the same set-up when school started again in the fall.

When it became clear that nothing would improve for her, I stopped caring about how she felt. Let her suffer.

Then I started to get mad.

It began slowly. I mocked her eye-rolling and whining (when my parents weren't around, of course). I avoided her, avoided talking to her, wanted her to shut up already. If I'd been able to get away with it, I would have smacked her every time she complained; I was getting almost as big as she was, and I began to realize that for the first time I could hurt her.

* * *

That summer I was glad to be out of Gardenview, away from the bullies and name-callers, and while my sister went to her skating classes I spent hours in my room reading, or lying in the back yard listening to CKGM on my parents' transistor radio. I was starting to like rock music a bit (except for the noisiest bands), and didn't mind when one of the louder groups interrupted the Fifth Dimension or the Beatles. Sometimes I went to St. Louis Park to watch a softball game or see the kids splashing around in the pool. For three weeks in August I went back to Camp B'nai Brith, and the only kids I knew from last summer weren't really friends. Stuart Kleiman and I became friends by default, and we always tried to be on the same baseball or rowing teams. But in a way I was glad he lived in Chomedey, and that at the end of camp we'd go our separate ways and not have to try any more. As we filed into the school bus to take us back to Montreal, we "accidentally" ended up sitting with other guys, and I spent the trip reading my comic books for the fifteenth time.

Things didn't go any better for me or Sheila that fall. My Grade 6 teacher was a chubby woman who wore tons of makeup, and her hair seemed to be cemented into a towering beehive. Miss Vineberg always squinted at us as if she needed glasses, and she couldn't seem to hear us much better. She didn't know how to control a class, so when the guys who sat in the back started talking—drawing others into their exchanges of fart noises or jokes about the teacher's name—almost the whole class would be mixed up in it before she'd notice and keep us all after school. And she made her preference for the girls obvious, so that I eventually stopped bothering to raise my hand to answer her questions. Joanne Copelovitch and Cheryl Glostein were her biggest pets.

Meanwhile, my sister started going to Sir Winston Churchill High, and was stuck with the same gang of girls from Gardenview she wanted nothing to do with, or who seemed to want nothing to do with her. She had to learn a whole new way of going to classes—a different room, with a different teacher, for each subject. The idea seemed bizarre and too grown-up for me to assimilate; I knew I would be going to high school in just a couple of years, but that was far enough away to make me think that I'd somehow learn to deal with it by then. What I knew of high school was what I saw on TV: kids old enough to drive, to date … a whole other world.

Sheila was nearly two years older than I was, and should have been able to cope. Instead, she complained constantly about the snobby kids, the World History teacher who did nothing but cover the blackboards with messily written notes that the class had to copy down, the kids who hung out in the basement "lounge" smoking and making fun of anyone not in their gang.

I stopped listening to her. She spent most of the time in her room with the door closed anyway, except when she came out to watch TV or eat. If she couldn't shut up, at least she could stay away, and take her whining with her.

In Grade 6, I had to deal with the same hostile kids from

the previous year. Some continued to call me "Spaceman." I stayed by myself in the schoolyard at recess, hoping no one would pick a fight.

But I finally made a friend during the preparations for a show Miss Vineberg wanted us to put on. She decided that we would teach the school about South America, and she distributed jobs to everyone based on what they were best at. I was good at science and history, so she had me research explorers. Rhonda Epstein and Richard Abrams wrote plays about Magellan and Simón Bolívar, and I would then be responsible for making sure the props and the ships painted on the backdrops were accurate. Miss Vineberg got very nervous that there'd be too many masts and sails, or that one of the explorers would use a telescope before they'd been invented. She taught me the word "anachronism" and made it sound like the worst sin in the world.

I chose to partner up with Paul Schneider, who was one of the nicer kids in the school. We'd gotten along all right when we worked on that Geography project. He was a little taller than me, with dark gray horn-rimmed glasses and the kind of longish hair I still couldn't see as proper for boys. His voice was changing already, so it was somewhere between what it was and what it was going to be, and went back up high at the strangest times.

"What colour are the ships supposed to be?" he asked me when we started work on the backdrops. "Does she want real colours or just outlines?"

"I don't know. Real, I guess." Knowing Miss Vineberg, silhouettes wouldn't be good enough.

"Then we'll have to get books on them." Our classroom

library had very little on ships. "I've got a card at the St. Laurent Public Library. My Dad takes me there every Saturday."

"*Every* Saturday?" I couldn't think of a more boring way to spend the weekend.

"Yeah, I do my homework there while he's reading the Jerusalem newspaper."

It would mean missing some of the Saturday afternoon shows, especially *Astro Boy*—that strange-looking, jumpy Japanese cartoon—but I had no choice. And in a way I was glad to have a reason to leave the house. On Saturdays Sheila was at her most unpleasant, though she seemed to quieten down by Saturday night and was almost happy as she watched *Jackie Gleason*. On weekdays she always managed to find some nasty word about the house, the neighbourhood, the kids, the slow bus serving our area that made it tough to go shopping downtown with Ma ... at Goyer we'd been a few blocks from the commuter train that ran under the mountain, so the trip had taken fifteen or twenty minutes. Now it took an hour.

At least she no longer wore that old tunic. The only girls in my class who still wore tunics were two Spanish cousins, Shirley and Sara; I imagined them coming from somewhere in South America, and figured they might be Miss Vineberg's inspiration for the show. They were assigned to the musical portion, singing folk songs. They also seemed to have no friends except each other. If my sister were still in Gardenview, I'd introduce them all to each other, bring them together, if only to give Sheila something to do besides complain.

* * *

Our work on the show required us to stay after school some-times—on those days when I didn't have Hebrew School —and I thought that was grossly unfair. After-school time belonged to me, not Miss Vineberg, and, even though the work was okay—almost fun, I thought she could have found class time for it.

Miss Vineberg supervised our work as often as she could, but of course she spent most of her time with the girls, even sitting beside them at a kid's desk when she had to. I couldn't get over seeing a teacher breaking through the line that normally separated her from the kids. For as long as I could remember, the teacher's and the pupils' worlds had always been, were *supposed* to be, separate. She looked simply *wrong* sitting there.

Paul and I determined the shapes and colours of our ships, and spread huge sheets of tissue-thin paper on the floor to draw and paint them. We used the classroom's supply of water-colours, which came in a metal box as a row of col-oured disks that always started clean and ended up with the colours spreading and mixing with each other. Paul knew how to draw—that was why he'd been given the job— and I watched him effortlessly sketch the ships (with per-spective and all) from the library books. Even when he drew the rigging his lines were mostly straight, and he added details like the outlines of the individual boards in the hulls. He knew where the water line would be (better than I could, anyway), so that the ships wouldn't sit absurdly high in the ocean. We had to be careful to get the order of our work right; first I painted the sky, complete with milky clouds, then we did the ship, and last I painted the ocean, covering the bottom of the sheet with dark blue swirls.

Thanks to our research we knew how many masts and sails Magellan's ships had, and what shape and relative size each of the sails was. Magellan had circumnavigated the globe, proving even more than Columbus did that the Earth was round. He'd had a rough trip, and even died along the way, but he hadn't been afraid to sail off to strange places. One of the books I read said that for Magellan, the Pacific Ocean during the 1500s was like outer space for us: a realm of unpredictable dangers, even (maybe) of alien lands, alien people, like the ones in my Dad's science-fiction magazines. I couldn't really see the comparison.

"Why'd you paint that green?" he asked, pointing to one of the masts."

"What do you mean? It's light brown, isn't it?"

"No, it's green."

"Oh." I was sure I'd chosen the right disk, but I took his word for it. "I always get those mixed up."

"Are you colour blind?"

"Of course not!"

But I was. The nurse had tested me earlier that year, showing me those cards with coloured spots; I could see no number at all on one of the cards, and thought it was some kind of trick. She told me I had a "mild red-green problem," which explained some things and didn't explain others. I'd always thought being colour blind meant you couldn't see colours at all—that you'd see the world in black and white, like our TV. Even though my problem was "mild" I couldn't afford to let anybody at school know about it. All I needed was for the kids to find out; they'd never leave me alone. I could hear them already: "What colour is this?" "Do you know what colour this is?" "Are you really *blind*?"

"Look, this one's brown, right?" I asked, pointing with my brush at another disk. He nodded. "So, okay!"

For the props, Paul and I scavenged material from home. I got my mother to supply an old clothesline for the rigging that Magellan's sailors would eventually have to eat when their food ran out. I tried painting it brown to make it look more nautical, but that was hopeless; I'd need gallons of paint. We used steel bookshelf brackets that Paul's father sold in his business as the blades of the cutlasses, and for trade goods my mother gave us some buttons from the collection she kept in a jar. The buttons made great coins and jewels. Paul's mother contributed some costume jewellery as well; she always wore earrings and gold brooches clipped to her coat whenever she went out. Paul's basement, unlike ours, wasn't an office but a real den, with a thick, comfortable chesterfield, glossy panelling, and a colour TV I watched with covetous wonder.

One thing that made the work bearable was knowing our parents would never see it. On TV shows like *The Brady Bunch*, parents came to watch their kids perform on stage, an idea that was too embarrassing to stomach. Our show would be for other classes only; we'd be their teachers for forty-five minutes. At least it was forty-five minutes we weren't spending on Arithmetic or Geography. I had no idea what the other kids in the school would think of Miss Vineberg's show, but I was glad I was not on stage myself. Cheryl Glostein became the star; she would be the narrator and sing one of the folk songs. I could see some of the other girls giving her grief for it—teasing her, laughing at her behind her back.

The weather grew colder; we got our first snowfall in early November. In South America summer was just beginning, which seemed impossible as the giant flakes fluttered by our classroom windows. I wasn't the only one watching the snow drift downward, and Miss Vineberg interrupted her spelling quiz to say: "What's the matter? Haven't you ever seen snow before?" She wanted us to believe that thousands of miles from us, people spent December and January sweltering under a fierce sun, and celebrated Christmas on beaches, in steaming jungles, in cities where the kids ran around without shoes, let alone boots. I knew about the tilt of the Earth, how the seasons worked in the two hemispheres. But she might as well have been talking about an alien planet filled with inverted, twisted marvels.

What with the show and Hebrew School I was almost never home before dark. Hebrew School was becoming less of a burden and more of a welcome break from the show; I would see my old Bedford School friends, and we'd catch up on news, compare what TV shows we were watching, trade hockey cards. By now I was beginning to realize that O-Pee-Chee printed dozens of Reg Flemings for every Jean Beliveau, so it was a waste of money to work at collecting the whole set. But I kept trying anyway.

"You still have to work on that stupid show?" Howard Cohen asked me again one afternoon, as he did every time we got together. We were standing outside the shul after Hebrew School as I waited for my father to pick me up. Howard was still wearing his fall coat from last year, the same blue nylon one with the white stripes, and it looked painfully tight on him.

"Yeah." I felt sorry for him and his public poverty. I wished I could do something about it.

"Can't you get out of it?"

"What? Lie?" He knew better than that. When a teacher wanted you to do something, you did it. Kenny Wasserman shoved him in the shoulder to tell him it was a dumb thing to say.

"Well, I don't know!" Howard said defensively, as in: *I was just asking.*

"It would take a miracle," I said. We'd just been taught for the fourth or fifth time about Chanukah. Every year the rabbi told us the origins of the holiday, and I never completely grasped the whole business of oil lamps. Still, I liked hearing about those days, the Bible times when miracles happened, when God could make magic happen when He wanted it to. My father's car pulled into the shul parking lot, and I waved goodbye to the guys. "See you!"

Dad had already opened the passenger-side door from the inside. "Come on, let's get going." I knew he was tired and getting impatient, but I didn't care. Moving had been his idea; my other late nights were Miss Vineberg's. It wasn't as if I'd had any say in the matter.

Sheila got home around the same time I did; as it turned out, Sir Winston Churchill had a skating club, and Sheila had joined even though she said it was too beginner for her. "Some of them don't even know how to stop right."

"Are they nice girls at least?" my mother asked, almost automatically, as she held out a hanger for Sheila's coat. Ma seemed to be expecting her to say no, but Sheila just shrugged. As if making friends didn't matter. My mother tightened her lips and gave up. She was starting to looked tired these days, too; she not only had to take care of the house, she also helped my father out with his bookkeeping, sorting invoices and even running the adding machine

Cheryl Glostein got on stage and began the narration, reading from a script Miss Vineberg had typed for her. "Hello, everybody, and welcome to Carnivale!" Those of us who weren't featured performers sat on the cold, polished gym floor pretending to be the audience; Miss Vineberg stood behind us, and I could hear her whispering under her breath, reciting the lines along with Cheryl. "Come with us now as we journey to the land of gauchos and rain forests, to the home of the mighty Amazon River, to South America!"

"Don't look just at me, Cheryl," Miss Vineberg said. "Look at everybody."

The show was divided into Peoples, Geography, History, and Culture. Cheryl introduced the peoples of South America, while pointing to a large map of the continent that had the different countries only partially painted in. Mark Yakovich, one of Paul's long-time friends, raced out onto the stage dressed as an Indian warrior, his costume a mass of beads and feathers. Shirley and Gloria walked on in long Peruvian dresses and derbies; Gloria's hat sat awkwardly on top of her glasses. For Geography, kids came out carrying samples of South American vegetation and foodstuffs, some made of paper and some real. Miss Vineberg had gone out to Dominion that afternoon to buy bananas and coffee beans; yarn stood in for South American wool. The show moved along quickly, and I figured the Grade 4s wouldn't get too bored.

When Cheryl announced that we would all be transported back in time for a look at South American history, I climbed up onto the stage. During the play, I just went wherever the other sailors did, following Magellan whose words, actions, even costume were closely based on the research Paul and I had done. The lights blinded me, so that

I could barely see our tiny audience, and everything seemed utterly phoney and overdone. I was glad when that play was over and I could go back to being a spectator.

As I sat down on the gym floor I stared at the backdrops Paul and I had painted, and then at the props we had constructed. Thanks to the bright lights, I could see everything much too well. Paul's drawing was still great, but my painting stank; the skies and oceans were streaked—you could see the brush strokes—and the props looked small and silly, like toys. Magellan and his crew did their best, but I couldn't stop looking beyond them at what Paul and I had done. The actors could say their lines as perfectly as they wanted to; the fact remained that I had turned their sky into patchwork, their ships into fuzzy brown hulks, their ocean into a mess of pale and dark stripes.

But Miss Vineberg applauded her actors, her singers, her dancers, as if nothing was wrong. She made it sound as if the show was fine, good enough, and nobody would notice the flaws anyway.

"That was wonderful, everybody," she said at the end. "We'll have our first performance on Thursday. Don't get nervous!"

She let us all go home then. Paul, Mark, and I left together. I kept waiting for Paul to tell me what he thought of our work—*my* work. But before taking off with Mark he didn't say anything except: "See you."

* * *

We held our performances for two Grade 4 classes and one Grade 3 class, and everything seemed to go okay. But I hated seeing the backdrops and props: the too-white rope, the tiny glass and ivory-coloured buttons you could barely see while Magellan referred to them as "valuable treasure." I cringed at the cutlasses, till I decided they needed to be covered with aluminum foil, and Paul and I spent an afternoon in his basement scotch-taping Reynolds Wrap to the blades. They now looked more like curved swords, and I was glad we'd managed to do something to salvage them. I looked out the window at the violet sky and blue snow banks. I couldn't help laughing to myself as I thought that somewhere an Indian or a gaucho was sweating in the blistering heat; a peasant in the rain forest was fanning himself thinking about Christmas.

As I put on my coat Paul asked in his squeaky voice: "You going home already? Hey, maybe my Mom will invite you to stay for supper."

"Oh." But I really had to get home, and anyway my mother needed more notice if I was going to have supper at a friend's house. If that's what he was. "Maybe tomorrow." Then I remembered Hebrew School. "Oh, I can't. What about Wednesday?" But we'd probably be busy then, too.

"Okay, I'll ask her."

"See you."

"Yeah, see you."

I walked home, huddling in my coat as I listened to my boots grinding the snow. My mother wanted me to make new friends; well, how was I supposed to do that? My afternoons belonged to everybody else. I would get them back, sooner or later. I went by St. Louis Park, and saw someone gliding around the ice rink. I knew instantly that it was Sheila.

The sun had just gone down, the lights weren't on yet, and the sky had turned everything—the snow, the ice, and her white skates—a bright blue. I stood by the rink and watched as she spun and leapt, flying and landing, her skates barely making a noise beyond a wavering hiss. My eyes were fixed on her blue skates, and I followed them as they veered and twisted, like something out of a movie or a dream. They didn't seem real, but they didn't seem wrong, either; they were alien and right, all at the same time.

I wanted to stay and wait for her and walk her home. But I was afraid she wouldn't want me to be there, and I wasn't sure what I'd say to her, if I could say anything at all. Part of me wanted to watch the magic forever, and part of me knew that she would stop eventually, and see me. I didn't know how I would be able to speak to her, and saying nothing would be even worse. I walked home, hoping I could make her understand someday, when I had more courage to tell her such things, to go that far.

Portals

THE BEST TOY I ever saw as a kid was an electric device owned by a guy I was friends with for only a few weeks. My mother usually knew all about my friends, since I would bring them over to the house or at the very least talk about them. But Erik Hakkonen was the sort of kid you didn't say too much about, because he did and owned dangerous things.

By the time I was thirteen I was pretty sure I was supposed to be outgrowing toys, but I had no intention of doing so. I didn't care what the boxes said: "Suitable for ages 5 and up" meant the contents ought to be too babyish for me. But I wanted my soldier collection to grow forever, and I didn't mind if my birthday gifts included another pack of G.I. Joe equipment from my grandmother, because she remembered that I owned an army G.I. Joe. I was still fascinated by the toys that I saw at the homes of friends and other kids—the ones I had to work with on school projects.

They owned things I saw advertised on TV but that we could never afford (or find room for): machine guns that made real sounds, Panel and Girder sets that produced entire cities, not just the single buildings of my Lego bricks, even a radio-controlled tank.

Erik had a Strange Change. It was essentially a toy-making machine that involved putting blocks of plastic onto a heater. The heater was topped with a futuristic clear cylinder like the glass dome that protected the clock on my grandmother's TV. I'd never owned a toy that you had to plug in; my mother would never let me fool around with electricity that way.

It was amazing watching the blue or red or yellow plastic shift and liquefy, grow arms and legs and head as it transformed magically into a dinosaur or alien beast. Despite the dome I could smell the melting plastic, and feel the heat radiate from all sides. I relished holding my hand just by the dome, feeling the heat burning through while the creature popped and slimed into birth.

* * *

Erik was almost one of the "cool" kids, which in Grade 7 meant that he wore a jean jacket and had shoulder-length hair. He was shorter than I was, and thus he was one of the shortest boys in my grade. He tried to hang out with the truly cool ones, the guys like Jeffrey Alter who spent recess sneaking puffs on cigarettes in a corner of the schoolyard, and the girls like Charlene Fein who watched them and giggled. I would sometimes see Erik smoke a little, too, but as soon as his back was turned Jeffrey and Benny Gold would mock his constant nodding.

Our teacher that year, Mrs. Rabinovitch, put Erik on a team with Paul Schneider and me on a book report. We had to come up with five pages on *Lord of the Flies*. Paul and I ended up doing most of the work, because Erik refused to read anything past the fourth chapter.

"It's boring after that," Erik said as we sat in Paul's dining room. "I like when Piggy gets killed. That's cool."

"So you didn't read anything?" Paul asked.

"Fuck, we don't need to."

"Yes, we do!" I said. I couldn't believe him. But I thought he had incredible guts. He was the sort who wouldn't hesitate to tell Mrs. Rabinovitch the very same thing. I imagined he was somehow connected to another world, a parallel universe, that made such behaviour seem okay. He was like those people in *Land of the Giants*, my new favourite show after *Lost in Space* and *Star Trek* were cancelled. They were flying in near-outer-space when they stumbled through a mysterious portal and ended up in a world of giant humans and objects, where all the rules were different, everything was distorted. There was never any explanation for where they were or how they got there—a source of unending frustration for me. It seemed as if Erik had found a similar alien world that made talking back to teachers and skipping school perfectly natural.

"I'll write up about the beginning," Erik said. "You write up the rest."

"That's not fair," Paul said. I nodded my agreement.

"So what's the big deal, anyway?" Erik sighed, making it clear we were being appalling sissies. I couldn't help thinking he was right, even as I knew I couldn't ever fail to do my homework.

Since we weren't getting anywhere with Erik, Paul and

I scribbled a few things down on our looseleaf sheets while Erik wrote a pathetically short paragraph on Piggy's death. He spent the rest of the time drawing guitars in the margins. Paul kept looking anxiously at Erik's sheet, afraid his pen would slip and he'd scratch up the glossy table. I could appreciate Paul's concern; his dining room was one of the most elegant places I'd ever sat in, with its polished oak and glass furniture, and the crystal and gold chandelier above. I hated to think of the room marred with scratches and stains.

"Fuck, I'm going home."

"Fine," I said, infuriated and relieved at the same time. We'd now get our work done, and quicker than if we still had him around our necks. And he'd stop being there making me feel like a goody-two-shoes.

"He's worthless," Paul said when he was gone. He pushed his glasses back up his nose; it always slipped when he bent over to do schoolwork. "Too bad we got stuck with him."

I shrugged. Part of me agreed, and the rest didn't know for sure.

We handed in the essay on Friday. For the final draft, Paul had incorporated whatever was worthwhile in Erik's paragraph, along with a few other comments we could convince ourselves were real contributions. After school, Erik came up to me in the yard and said: "Hey, want to see something cool?"

"Sure."

He led me to his apartment building on Ward, just south of my house and not far from the Metropolitan Expressway where it met the Trans-Canada. His building was white-brick, like the majority of my Legos, and was the sort

I would have loved to live in since it seemed so modern and clean. Science-fiction books and magazines always showed cities made up of shiny tall buildings, gleaming amidst carefully tended parks, as silver rockets arced overhead.

The lobby had a more mod chandelier than Paul's: silver and glass in criss-crossing geometric shapes. We stood before the elevators waiting for one to come down from the tenth floor, Erik shifting his weight from foot to foot. "Fuck, come *on*!" I watched the numbers light up one after the other, enjoying the idea of living in a place like this. We'd always lived in duplexes before buying the house. No elevators—just speckled-stone stairs.

The elevator finally arrived, and we had to wait for a tall old man to shuffle his way out, a shopping bag from Esposito's in one hand. "Okay!" Erik cried with exasperation as soon as the way was clear, and I cringed, since I was pretty sure the old man could hear him. The elevator ride was smooth and quiet, as if operating on anti-gravity rather than cables.

We got off on the seventh floor, and I hoped that from this height I'd get a great view of Montreal from his windows. He led me to the apartment at the end of the hall, unlocked and swung open the door, and I took a quick glance around. The floor was covered with thick gray carpet, and the living room was straight ahead; beyond it was a wall made almost entirely of window and a balcony door. The blue-and-yellow-striped chesterfield was bare of plastic. Before going into Erik's room I moved past the chesterfield and kidney-shaped coffee table to take a quick peek through the plate glass. As it turned out, his apartment faced north, meaning I could see nothing but stretches of flat houses —a sea of roofs—and roads.

"Come on! This is great. Oh, that's my mother's room over there."

On his bedroom door was a poster of Jim Morrison: unshaven, staring out with a sombre expression as if he'd just been insulted, his long greasy hair hanging down.

"Fuck, isn't he *dirty*?" Erik said, giggling.

"Is your mother home?" I asked. It struck me I hadn't seen any grownups around; Erik was completely alone. I'd never been to a guy's house when there wasn't at least somebody there, even an older brother or sister.

"No. Why? She works."

"Oh."

Then he wasn't all that rich, if his mother had to work. I figured only some women had to go out to work: those who weren't married, like my cousin Ruth, or those who lived in my grandparents' old neighbourhood near St. Lawrence. My Aunt Ellen still lived there, and when we visited her I saw around me a world where everybody was one step away from utter deprivation.

Yet here he had his electric toy, something I couldn't dream of actually owning. He plugged it into a wall socket by the bed, and there I saw a guitar case standing upright against the moulding around the closet door. "You play the guitar?"

"Yeah. Later. Check this out. It's so cool."

We spent an hour making little rectangles of coloured plastic into dinosaurs, then watching them revert to their original blocks. I felt it was the coolest thing I'd ever seen.

"There's something like this on TV," I said. "Creepy Crawlers. Junk like that."

"Yeah. You get a Thingmaker and can make bugs, soldiers, stuff like that."

"Soldiers?" Now there was a truly glorious idea. Make your own soldiers? I could fill up my armies at will, infinitely, limited only by how much plastic I could afford. I had to have one.

"Yeah. Big ones you can bend." He showed the size with his hands: about five inches.

That was too bad; I was hoping I could create hundreds, even thousands of the three-inch ones that made up the bulk of my collection. Still, the possibilities …

Even though we used the tweezers that came with the set, we burned our fingers a few times, and the side of my forefinger refused to stop hurting no matter how much cold water I poured over it. I didn't mind too much, although Erik screamed, "Shit!" each time he slipped and made contact with the heater. I thought there was something heroic about getting those burns.

The apartment door opened with a *clumph*. Erik went out into the front hall. "Hey, *Clara*."

"I told you not to call me that!"

I was stunned. Had he really called her by her first name? I was sure she'd kill him — and I didn't want to be around for it. But instead she asked calmly: "What are you up to?"

I went to the doorway. She had long blond hair and looked simultaneously older and younger than my own mother. Her eyes were sharply lined, but she was immensely pretty. And I couldn't imagine my own mother wearing a dress that short. She clutched a paper grocery bag. "Hello," she said to me. "And what's your name?"

"Lawrence."

"Nice to meet you, dear." She had on pink stockings,

and I stared as she headed for the kitchen. "Do you want to stay for supper?" she called.

"No, that's okay." I didn't think I could just call home and ask permission at the last minute like that. I figured she was just being polite anyway, like my mother when she dealt with some of her neighbours. She made insincere invitations, then said afterward how glad she was they turned her down.

"Well," Mrs. Hakkonen said. "We're going to be eating soon."

"You better go, eh?" Erik said. He was right: It was five o'clock already. I got my school bag, and as I was leaving his room I saw the guitar case and thought I could invite myself over some time, listen to him play it. Maybe I'd learn how to play it myself.

I took the elevator down, torn in a thousand directions. Erik was a bad kid, the kind my mother always feared I would befriend: someone bound to lead me into a life of undescribed depravity. When she warned me about such things I resented her distrust, because I'd always been so consciously *good*, doing everything possible to avoid trouble. If I told her about Erik, I'd confirm everything she'd ever said, and I would never hear the end of it. Yet I wouldn't stop being friends with him.

And I thought about Mrs. Hakkonen, and wondered what it must be like to have a mother who looked like the ones on TV: like Elizabeth Montgomery on *Bewitched*, like Florence Henderson on *The Brady Bunch*. My friends' mothers, and my own mother's B'nai Brith friends, were overweight, ugly, often loud. When my sister and I were younger and still shared a room, every time my mother played host

to her Rumoli-playing group the women screeched so loudly
we had to keep our bedroom door closed so we could sleep.
We insisted on having a lamp brought in to keep the room
from being too dark, and my father had to set up an elaborate system of his manila folders to keep it from shining in
our eyes.

As I walked home from Erik's, I decided this was one
secret I could keep from my mother. I didn't want to be friends
with him anyway, not in the real sense. But I thought he
could teach me things, maybe even how to cross the bound-
ary, pass through the portal he'd found, if only for a minute.

* * *

I didn't dare ask my parents for a Thingmaker. We'd bought
the house just recently, and my father was working for himself, trying to get enough bookkeeping work to pay for it.
Of course, I had no idea how much money we had, or needed, but I knew that we weren't rich. I wasn't sure I wanted
the responsibility of having an electric toy anyway. What if
something went wrong? What if I burned the house down?
I knew I wouldn't be that stupid, but I couldn't help imagining a fiery disaster.

So I didn't obsess about the Thingmaker, but I did think
about Mrs. Hakkonen. I pictured scenarios where I'd have
to stay over at Erik's place overnight, and the things that
might happen: accidents and deliberate violations. One
night, as I lay in bed, I created a whole storyline: bedtime
and bath, loving smiles …

Oh, my God!

I couldn't believe it; it was as if I'd become a baby again, wetting my bed like a little brat. Everything felt and smelled wrong, and as I tried to mop up with wads of Kleenex I was desperate to understand and block it all out at the same time. It wouldn't happen ever again, and no one could ever find out ... was I sick? Or was all my desire for toys causing me to go backwards in time? Like that stupid Strange Change, which the commercials were calling "The Time Machine" because dinosaurs came out of it. I was going backward—growing *down*—and all the wrong things my body had been doing lately were a rotten betrayal. I'd had sex education in Health in Grade 6, so I understood the hair and the changed voice. But this was something else, something no one had ever told me. That it could all go horribly wrong, that you could get caught in a time loop and go in all directions.

I ran to the bathroom, hoping no one would see me and my pyjamas. Fortunately, my parents were down in the basement, watching the TV news where the noise wouldn't disturb us. My sister's door was closed and she was probably fast asleep. I slammed the Kleenex down furiously into the toilet, then panicked when I realized I might clog the thing and cause a flood. I rinsed my pyjama bottoms in the sink, washed myself with one of those little facecloths we never used but had stored under the sink. I squeezed the water out of my bottoms.

Now what? I hadn't brought another pair with me.

I had to put the bottoms back on, endure the cold damp cloth clinging to my legs and behind as I ran back to my room to change. In my top dresser drawer I had an old pair whose bottom had a stretched-out elastic waist, and put that on as I draped the wet pyjamas over my chair. All I could think was, thank God my mother would just knock on my door to wake me up the next morning; she no longer came in to shake me. I prayed that the bottoms would be dry by then, so I could put them on and no one would be the wiser.

I'd forgotten to flush the toilet.

I lay awake, seemingly for hours, wondering what the hell was wrong with me.

* * *

I did begin to understand what had happened, but it took some time. Meanwhile, I tried to be friends with Erik, despite how difficult he made it. I went over to his apartment once more, again while his mother was at work—much to my disappointment and relief. He didn't want to play with the Strange Change again; instead, he pulled a portable phonograph—the kind with the detachable lid that held the speaker—from under his bed and set it up on his bed. In the bottom drawer of his desk he had a stack of 45s.

"You got to listen to these," he said as he jammed the red plastic 45 adapter down the spindle.

He turned up the volume full-blast and played the records one by one as we sat on the floor: Most were by the Doors, some by Janis Joplin, some by the Rolling Stones. The louder and harsher, it seemed, the better. It wasn't the kind of music I preferred, but I wanted desperately to like it. Or at least understand why anybody would.

"Fuck, isn't that *great*?" He nodded to Jim Morrison's beat.

"Sure." I looked over at the guitar case.

"What?" He followed my gaze and reached for the case. He dragged it to where we sat and opened it. Inside was a blond-wood guitar gleaming in the light coming through his window. He pretended to play it, following the record's chords and bearing down hard as the song reached its climax.

"Can you play anything for real?" I asked once the song was over.

"Yeah! Of course!"

"Prove it."

So he strummed away on something I didn't recognize. It sounded like music, although I'm not sure he played everything perfectly. Then he handed it to me.

"Here. Try it."

I did. I had no idea what I was doing, but I plucked at the strings anyway. I didn't know that I had to finger the strings, too; Erik tried to show me but I couldn't do it. So I just strummed away, producing a soulful sequence of notes that seemed utterly deep to me.

"Fucking great!"

I heard the front door open. I'd stayed too long again, and there she was, out in the foyer. I watched her through the doorway. Another short dress, and this time panty-hose. She raised her knees to pull off her shoes. Erik went out, but before he could say a word she said: "Got another call today! I don't need this!"

"*Clara.*" His tone was soothing, but that's all. Even the way he stood there seemed to be a challenge.

"I told you to stop calling me that! And I'm not going to put up with this crap any more!"

"Who cares?"

"At work! They're calling me at work about you!"

I tried to withdraw out of her sight. My movement called her attention to me.

"Hello, dear," she said, as if nothing were wrong, nothing had happened. The last I saw of her before I slid back behind Erik's door was as she walked toward her own bedroom on the other side of the living room.

"I gotta go," I said. I hurriedly retrieved my bag and practically ran out of the apartment. I even forgot to say goodbye.

For the next couple of weeks I saw Erik only once in a while at school. He was usually going to or from the principal's office. One time his mother came to the school to get him; she had broken the invisible barrier between parents and the world of the school. There we stood in the yard just after the lunch bell, and Mrs. Hakkonen emerged from the door nearest the office with Erik in tow. She was actually dragging him across the yard by the sleeve of his spring jacket, and I was sure I saw him swearing quietly at her. On they went to a white car parked awkwardly at the curb, with one of its wheels on the sidewalk. She opened the passenger side door and practically shoved him inside, then went around to her own side, got in, and instantly started the engine. Then they sped off, the car bouncing as its right front tire hit the road.

I wanted to feel sorry for him, to hope that he'd get away with it again—whatever it was. But instead I felt as if this was the proper end of things, as if that other world beyond the portal had finally disintegrated.

* * *

I spoke to him only once more, when we were both going to Sir Winston Churchill High. He'd joined the kids who hung out in the basement "lounge," smoking and skipping classes—probably all of them. I didn't see him unless I was on my way toward the Metalwork or Woodwork rooms. I'd try to catch his eye but only got a nod once in a while.

Then one day we were in the schoolyard. I was nervously fingering the keys in my pocket; to my shame, my mother had just recently gone back to work to help pay for the house. My father kept saying how bad the economy was now, how his clients were starting to go bankrupt, how inflation was killing everything. I hated the fact that she wasn't there when I got home. By then my sister was in CEGEP, and came home at weird hours; but I was still on a regular school schedule, and needed my own set of keys to get into my empty house.

Erik stood alone against the fence, and I wondered where his long-haired friends were. He had a moustache, or the beginnings of one, and was wearing an army jacket with a Scandinavian flag patch on the shoulder—I could never get straight which was which. He looked at me and smiled, nodding his hello.

"Fuck, hi!"

"Hi. What's up?"

"Nothing. Want to see something?"

"What?"

He opened his right hand. In it were two yellow and white pills. They looked like the plastic Mexican Jumping Beans we used to buy as kids; we'd hold them in our hands till they heated up, then watch amazed as they skipped around on our palms. Magic.

"Crazy, eh?" He giggled.

"Yeah." I looked past him, as if there were something on the other side of the fence.

"Fuck."

"Okay. See you."

I walked out of the schoolyard toward home, and tightened my grip on the briefcase I now carried my stuff in. With my other hand I held onto the keys, to keep them from jingling too loudly.

Passover Order

AFTER FOUR YEARS of Hebrew School, I found that I knew very little Hebrew, and not much more about the rest of the things the rabbis tried to teach us. Even though it was called Hebrew School, we weren't really there to learn the language, just how to read the letters so that we could recite blessings from the prayer book and then, more importantly, sing the Bible passage at our Bar Mitzvahs.

Most of what we learned involved the holidays: who did what to the Jews and the miracles that saved us. At the time I wanted to learn more than that, but we kept going over the same territory, each year hearing yet again the stories of Purim, Chanukah, and Passover. It was like arithmetic at regular school; every year we went over the same rules about multiplication and division, and the teachers would tell us all about Venn diagrams as if we'd never heard of them before. Hebrew School was supposed to be different, and I thought that it was where I'd find out the most important things, the ones that would count while we were being judged by God. But Rabbi Steiner and Rabbi Friedman were satisfied to just narrate the evils of Haman and Pharaoh, then have us write compositions (in English!) telling the stories again to prove we'd been listening.

On Passover, though, the rabbis handed out *Haggadah*s for free and tried to lead us through their instructions for holding *seder*s. But it was clear as Rabbi Friedman rushed through his talk that we weren't really supposed to be memorizing the steps along the way. He'd show us the pages with the blessing over the bitter herbs or the long answers to the Four Questions, and had us read them over more to see whether we could read Hebrew than to teach us the procedures themselves.

To me, the most worthwhile parts of the *Haggadah* were the drawings. One picture showed where on the *seder* table all the different foods were supposed to be, with rough sketches of shank bones and cups of wine. Elsewhere were drawings of ancient Hebrews in long robes marching across the desert sand behind Moses. They followed him because he was supposed to know where he was going; he'd gotten them out of Egypt thanks to God's help, and was leading them to Israel. It was their own fault, Rabbi Friedman told us, that they ended up wandering the desert for forty years. If they had obeyed God's laws, paid attention to His rules, they would have found their way home right away. On maps, the Sinai Peninsula looked so small, and it wasn't as if there were lots of mountains or forests to get lost in. It seemed ridiculous to me that the Hebrews could have gotten lost, even with God's anger deflecting them. It took so little to get from one end to the other—the distances seemed so short, especially compared to Canada—and at the same time so little to send them wandering around those burning, wide-open spaces like blind people.

For me, Hebrew School was something to endure after regular school, not attend instead of it. But my cousin David had gone to Young Israel, a "real" Jewish school where all they did was study Hebrew and the Jewish laws—as far as I could tell, anyway. There were even times I considered, though not very seriously, asking my parents to switch me over to a Jewish school; I might have transferred if it hadn't meant leaving all my friends behind. And when we moved to Ville St. Laurent, afternoon Hebrew School was my only remaining contact with my friends from my old neighbour-hood, and nothing was going to make me give them up alto-gether. Still, as I coped with all the meaningless Canadian history and celebrations of Christian holidays at Bedford School and then at Gardenview, I felt as if I was wasting my time, missing something important, something that David and other kids who went to Jewish schools were learning. Not just being told—actually *learning*.

I never forgot watching him at a wedding I went to when I was small. My parents, my sister, and I sat in the *shul* not far from David and his witch-like and much older sister Ruth, who never smiled and had a bent back that made her seem only slightly less than towering. As the service that preceded the ceremony went on, David followed along with the others, even keeping up with the fast portions when the congregation muttered Hebrew at an amazing speed. He and the others could read Hebrew more quickly than I could read English, and they zipped through prayers that

became, to my ears, a meaningless buzz. I desperately wanted to be able to do that.

* * *

By the spring of 1970, I had had my Bar Mitzvah and my
parents decided that I no longer needed to go to Hebrew
School. I'd graduated from the *shul*'s school anyway, and the
only thing left for me was to go into some sort of advanced
Torah study class or even a Yeshivah.

"You aren't planning to become a rabbi, are you?" my mother asked. We were sitting at the kitchen table, the same one
we'd had in our old duplex and that to me always looked so
odd in its new setting. The swirls in the gleaming formica
top kept reminding me of the old place, where I thought
everything had been better.

I had no answer for my mother. It all seemed so unfair;
the Hebrew School was my last link with my old school
friends, and on top of that I wasn't sure what I was supposed
to do now. For years, I'd been thinking that I ought to study
something Jewish, even though I never liked the idea of
spending after-school time in yet another school. The problem was all the time I'd wasted in regular school singing
hymns ... And I knew something else: Hebrew School cost
money, and we'd just bought a house, and unless I could
come up with very good reasons for making them spend
the money on me—say, that I really *was* planning to be a
rabbi—going any further made no sense. In the silence, my
father's stew *blupped* on the stove.

"Anyway," she said, "you're going to high school next
year. Everything's going to be different."

"Yeah," I replied, although I couldn't see how. I hated the kids around here, and now I'd be stuck with them for four more years. I hadn't made many friends in St. Laurent; neither had she.

"What can I tell you?" she asked with a shrug.

It was almost Passover, and the following Saturday she went into the Esposito Brothers supermarket in the St. Louis Shopping Centre to make her Passover order. I dreaded Passover, because the foods tasted consistently awful. We had to give up our cereals, our bagels, our *challah*, and replace them with tasteless *matzoh*s that required a sweeping layer of butter and strawberry jam, or pimento cheese, to make them edible. We had to have only "Kosher for Passover" foods, which meant different brands, some of them Israeli. Humpty-Dumpty potato chips were out in favour of Mad Hatter; sugary jelly candies in the shape of fruit slices that made my teeth ache for a different reason; no more Betty Crocker or Duncan Hynes cake mixes, or my mother's honey cake, but hard *mandelbrot* that made you think you were going to break your teeth. They even managed to make apple juice taste terrible.

There were only two things that made Passover bearable. The first was the Israeli chocolate syrup to make chocolate milk; it tasted better than Quik and mixed more easily. The other was the Montreal tradition of celebrating the end of Passover by going to Yangtze's Chinese restaurant on Van Horne. After a week of enduring all those dry, tasteless, or sour foods, we could enjoy the egg rolls, the glorious pineapple chicken that my mother, after some years, figured out how to make, and the spare ribs. We would either order from Yangtze's or go out to the restaurant. I always preferred ordering in, because if we went there we would have to line up, and then once we were seated my parents would inevitably meet lots of people they knew (I noticed there were never any Chinese people eating there), mainly my mother's friends from B'nai Brith. "Shirley, hi!" "Jack, what's doing?" "You look like you've had enough—look at that pot!" They would all start chatting loudly, meaning even further delays in ordering, and breaking the sort-of fast.

"Come on," my sister or I would whine, "I'm *hungry*."

"Okay, okay," my mother would say. "I'll talk to you later, Ethel." And then the waiters in their little red jackets would take our orders, disappear for an agonizing time, and return bearing ceramic platters full of shimmering wonders.

Now that we were in St. Laurent, we were well beyond Yangtze's delivery area, so ordering in was no longer an option. I yearned for that line-up stretching out the door and down the street toward the Van Horne Shopping Centre, where the Brown Derby restaurant would also be packed; I yearned for the round table with its white tablecloth still bearing pale stains; I yearned for the chicken fried rice, the chicken soo guy, even the won ton soup I only had a taste of because I wanted to save room for the "real" food.

But that time seemed an eternity away as the delivery men carried the boxes from Esposito through our front door, and all I saw poking up out of the (ironically enough) Frosted Flakes cartons were the Manischewitz and Streit's labels. My heart sank. Where in the Bible did it say we had to eat bad-tasting kosher apple sauce, with little pieces of core in it that jammed up between your teeth? Or rubbery Israeli chocolate-covered marshmallows?

It was my duty to put away the weekly supermarket order,

and my mother had already emptied the shelves, moving all the real food into storage in the closet of the basement room that my father was using as an office. As I reluctantly arranged the boxes and cans in the kitchen cupboards, my mother said: "David will be leading the *seder*."

"He's coming?" My father and I had always tried our best to do something like a *seder*, but that mainly involved saying a couple of *brochah*s—blessings—and my singing the main question a kid is supposed to ask on Passover: "*Mah nishtanah halilah hazeh, mikol halailot?*" Why is this night different from all other nights? I knew the answer, because my Hebrew School teachers had told me a thousand times; my father didn't have to read out the long passages from the *Haggadah*, and couldn't have done so, anyway.

I was glad David was coming, to save our *seder* and make it proper. I could imagine him doing everything, and saying it all correctly. By then, David was in his final year at Herzliah, which was supposed to be a great Jewish school. I envied him mightily. That sounded like a place where Jewish kids were supposed to go, not just whatever Protestant School Board of Greater Montreal high school was closest. I was going to go to Sir Winston Churchill High.

But while I looked forward to having David there, I felt bad about it, too. We shouldn't have had to bring him in to lead our *seder*; by now, after four years of Hebrew School, *I* should have been able to do that. Why had we spent so much time reviewing old crimes by Persian kings or even what Hitler had done? God had saved us, Moses had saved us, all that was over. And I still couldn't read Hebrew properly or light the Chanukah candles without reading the blessings out of a book or run a *seder*. Something was terribly wrong.

On the first night of Passover, David came with Ruth and their parents Uncle Nat and Aunt Tillie. Even though I'd had my growth spurt already David was still much taller than me; he took after Uncle Nat, who towered over Aunt Tillie and my mother. The last time I'd seen my aunt and uncle was at my Bar Mitzvah. I wasn't sure why we saw them so seldom, but that was fine by me, as Nat had a gruff, loud voice that had always scared me as a little kid. Ruth and David visited us sometimes without them; Ruth was around my mother's age and they liked to get into long conversations I had to interrupt to get whatever I might need. When they weren't sitting over tea at the kitchen table, or out on the balcony (at my old duplex), they were on the phone discussing other people: B'nai Brith women, relatives, and so on. Occasionally they would switch to Yiddish, and at least then I didn't get distracted from TV-watching or other activities by their gabbing, because I couldn't understand them at all.

"Hey, there!" Uncle Nat yelled at me as he pulled off his overcoat. They brought the outside cold in with them, and it clung to their clothes and hands. Uncle Nat insisted on shaking my hand, and his grip was always painfully hard. "Been keeping out of trouble?"

"Yeah—"

At that moment Aunt Tillie grabbed my chin. "*Oy*, so tall!" I could smell her lipstick as she planted a kiss on my forehead. "When did he get so tall?"

I thought my mother would say something to that, but it was clearly a question you weren't supposed to respond to. I was learning that sometimes people asked questions just to ask, and didn't want or expect you to answer.

"And Sheila! My God!" Uncle Nat and Aunt Tillie admired her height, her dress, the fact that she was already at Sir Winston ("So young and in high school already!"). The women then headed into the kitchen, where the table had been set for a proper *seder*. My mother's Passover platter, with compartments marked off showing what food belonged where, sat in the middle of the table fully prepared with the shank bone, the egg, a small bowl of horseradish, celery stalks, and the rest of the strange foods. Wine glasses stood at our places, and I would be expected to drink some of the horrible Manischewitz wine or maybe the kosher grape juice that wasn't much better.

David shook my hand, too, but he did it gently. His hair was a bit longer now, and he was growing sideburns; he'd been to a rock concert somewhere in the Eastern Townships, I'd heard. From what I'd seen of movies of Woodstock, a rock concert sounded unthinkably decadent. "How's school?" he asked.

"Okay. I'm almost finished elementary school now."

"Yeah! So where are you going next year?"

"Sir Winston Churchill," I said. Did the kids at Herzliah walk around with *yarmulke*s on their heads all day? Were they expected to pray all the time? Now I began to wonder how much I'd want the burden, the constant pressure to be correct. But I couldn't help feeling ashamed, the same way I felt when I saw Hassids in Outremont who were so properly *orthodox*.

David shrugged, then absently rubbed his stomach. "Okay. Any more problems with store owners?"

I laughed. He always asked me that. "No, not any more."

When I was a little kid, I bought my hockey cards at

Aaron's Variety down Wilderton Street. Aaron was a shrivelled little man who looked a bit like Johnny Bower. I hated him because he would always serve grown-ups first, no matter where I was in the line at the counter; even if I was first, Aaron would immediately stop serving me if a grown-up walked in. "What can I do for you?" he'd ask over my head, as if I wasn't there.

I told David about that during one of his visits, and he said: "Oh, really? What a *shmeggegi*." We went to look at my card collection. "Every time you go to buy some he treats you like that?"

"Yeah."

He thumbed through the cards, concentrating on the Canadiens. I was still missing Jean Beliveau, but I had Gump Worsley and Ted Harris, two of my other favourites.

He said: "Listen, why don't you go down to Aaron's and get us something?" He reached into his pocket and pulled out some dimes. "Do you like Cherry Blossom?"

"Yeah." They weren't my favourite, mainly because you got only a single big piece rather than a number of pieces that you could savour one by one, and I wasn't fond of the maraschino cherry itself. But I loved the rich cherry sauce that poured out when you bit into the chocolate.

"Get a couple from Aaron's, eh?"

I went down to the store. I looked at the candy display in front, locating the little yellow boxes beyond the Dairy Milks and Rosebuds. Sure enough, Aaron served me last, letting two women who were buying cigarettes get ahead of me. I made a face at him as I handed over the money, and left without saying thank you.

I returned home thinking David and I would eat our Cherry Blossoms together while we discussed the cards I had and the ones I needed. But to my surprise he went out on the balcony, where no one was around. I ate mine while admiring the substantial stack of cards held together with an elastic band; if only I had the whole set, and it made a perfect stack, one just the right size ...

"Hey, Lawrence." David stood behind me holding his box. "Guess what?"

"What?"

"There was nothing in it."

I stared at him. "*What?*"

"There was nothing in it. Take it back and get another one."

"There was nothing in it?"

"Yeah. I thought it was a bit light. There was no Cherry Blossom in it." He opened the box to show me.

Sure enough it was empty. I couldn't understand it, but things like that happened. My father bought a science fiction magazine once, and instead of the first fifty pages it contained pages 51-100 printed twice. When I was younger and something like that happened, I thought the problem was with me, that I was missing something, that grown-ups didn't make mistakes and that there must be a reason for such things that was beyond me. I knew better now. Aaron had cheated us.

"Go back and get another one, eh?"

That's what I did. I stood before his counter and held out the box to him. "It was empty," I said, holding my temper but letting him know by my expression.

"Eh? What are you talking about?" He looked inside.

"It was empty. There wasn't anything in it."

He stared at me, speechless for a moment. "Come on! You have the nerve to come to my store—"

But he saw I was telling the truth. He snatched a box from the display and tossed it at me. "Here, get going."

I brought the Cherry Blossom home, and David smiled as he took it. "Good!" he said, when I told him what happened. "That'll teach him." He opened the box in front of me and showed me that this one was full. "Here, you take it."

Now, every time I saw him he asked me if I still had trouble with store owners. In the back of my mind I was pretty sure what really happened, but if neither of us said anything it wouldn't be confirmed, and we could go on as if what was said back then was true.

I was no longer collecting hockey cards, but I still kept the ones I'd collected over the years. We went to my room and I showed him the set of black-and-white autographed photos of the Canadiens I got years before when I sent to the Forum a picture I did in Art class of Beliveau scoring a goal. "Jeez, these are great," he said, handling them with great care. The autographs were real, not printed. Sadly, the current crop of Canadiens weren't winners; it looked like Boston would win the Stanley Cup again, and again …

"Okay, come on!" my mother called, and we went into the kitchen. She'd put all the leaves into the kitchen table, and it stretched right to the walls of the dining area. We squeezed into our positions. At one end of the table, my mother had set up a pile of *yarmulke*s saved over the years from various weddings and Bar Mitzvahs—including my own—and the men made their selections; I used the gray velvet one I'd worn at my Bar. David took up his place at the head of the table, where my mother had placed the *Haggadah* I'd gotten from Hebrew School, and from then on, David took over. When it was my turn, even though I was too old for it I asked the questions, singing the main one and then saying the others because I didn't know the tunes or whether I was even supposed to sing them at all. Why is this night different from all other nights? Because for a change the *seder* would be done properly. I'd failed miserably, though it wasn't really my fault, but David saved us.

Maybe a bit too well.

The *seder* went on and on, and I got hungrier and hungrier. It seemed as if the answer to my question would never end, while I didn't understand a word of it. My father read from the *Haggadah*, slowly, when David prompted him. Even my mother said a few words. We hadn't bothered with the search for *hametz*, when you were supposed to find every scrap of leavened bread in the house and get rid of it; the cereal and other non-kosher foods would remain in the basement, so there was no point in pretending to "clean" the house. But even so the ceremony took forever. I could see my father squirming, and I exchanged a look with my sister when I was able to find where in the *Haggadah* we were: barely halfway through.

We had to lift the plate and find the *afikoman*, the hidden piece of *matzoh*; we had to dip the celery in the salt water; we had to sip the wine, eat the horseradish (I refused more than an almost invisible speck of it), say *brochah* after *brochah*. David rushed through the story of Passover, his words blurring together, right up to the stories of the curses and miracles, the things that happened at midnight. That was when the miracles happened, when magic ruled the world of the Hebrews pictured in the *Haggadah*. No matter what happened, no matter what the anti-Semitic kings and Pharaohs did, God saved us, and proved who His favourite children really were. Things always worked out in the end, because they had to.

At the end of the service, David asked me: "Do you want to sing those songs?"

They were kids' songs that were printed at the back of the *Haggadah*, like "Chad Gadya," which meant "One Goat." It was a build-up song, like "The House That Jack Built." Singing it had been one of the fun parts of Hebrew School and B'nai Brith camp. But I was too old for it now. "No, let's just eat."

"Amen," Uncle Nat said. We laughed, and David nodded.

"You did a nice job," my father said, and my mother agreed. David thanked them, then waited with the rest of us as my mother brought in the real food—or the food that was as real as it got.

As I ate the brisket, softening my piece of *matzoh* in the juice, I couldn't help wondering: Even if I'd known how to run the *seder*, would I have wanted to? The answer should have been obvious, but it wasn't. I watched David eat, his hand periodically dropping to his belly as if he was already full—even at the beginning—and I felt a thousand things rushing through me. I should have been the one to lead things, not him; or it should have been my father, who'd never gone to Hebrew School but maybe should have; I was grateful to David for saving us, and making sure that at least one of our Passovers went the way it was supposed to; and I didn't want to have a proper *seder* again. Maybe if I'd understood the words ... yes, it was true that my *Haggadah* contained a translation, but that wasn't the part you spoke aloud. You said it all in Hebrew, and as David's voice burred away, I'd found nothing in it that meant anything to me, one way or another. It was like my mother's Yiddish conversations, a blank noise.

It shouldn't have been like that, but it was.

We ate a lot, because we were all really hungry, but it still didn't seem like a supper. There was no dessert, except for a plateful of those jelly candies I couldn't bear to eat. I was already thinking of Passover's end, when we'd get back to normal.

As David and the others were leaving, much later that night, I shook his hand, for once making sure that I was the one that initiated the gesture. I wanted to thank him, but I also wanted to let him know something I could barely understand myself: I wasn't just a kid any more, I could say these things without prompting from my parents, I wasn't sure I needed his help any longer. I don't know what he took from the way I grabbed his hand and squeezed it gently. Probably nothing. He was a grown-up now himself, part of a different world, like someone who had gone to a distant land that I could barely imagine coming to myself. But he'd never really treated me like a kid.

* * *

I only understood his motions at the dinner table, when he'd held his stomach, a couple of years later. Nobody knew then what was inside, growing away in silence. I'd always been told that the Jewish General was the best hospital, but the doctors there kept misdiagnosing him, probably because they wouldn't see him right: He was a young man, he couldn't have things like that.

We saw his parents far more often after David was admitted; they came over for meals, or we were at their house or at the hospital. My mother and Ruth spent so much time together it was as if Ruth had moved in again, as she had when she babysat for us while my grandfather was sick years before. Now things were turned around.

I kept waiting for David to be released, cured or at least better, because I didn't fully understand and couldn't imagine anything else. When the phone call came, my mother stared aimlessly toward the kitchen, receiver clutched in her hand. It took hours before she could talk to us, tell us what Aunt Tillie had told her.

"There was nothing left inside of him. They operated and there was nothing left. Nothing they could do."

I wanted her to be making it up. I wanted her to be saying it in Yiddish, or Hebrew, or another language she might know that would explain everything, answer all the questions, and mean nothing to me.

War Games

T O THIS DAY, when I hear the word "soldier" I think of the toy soldiers I had when I was a kid. I could easily divide them into two armies: the green "Combat" American soldiers on one side, and then all the rest, which I called the Allies, made up of Russians, British, multi-coloured cowboys and Indians, and whatever others my Dad had bought me over the years. My battles involved firing Lego bricks at both sides in alternating volleys till one side was unable to field a respectable line. The Americans were always the good guys, and nearly always won.

Strangely, the word "army" has for a long time made me think of something quite different: real young men in loose-fitting uniforms. Part of the reason was the news reports we saw almost every night about the Vietnam War and the American army; I couldn't think of the wounded men I saw carried on stretchers as "soldiers." Mostly, though, it was because I actually saw an army once, on an October day a few weeks before my fourteenth birthday. That year, "army" became a dark word for me, as if it held weight and danger. The men I saw didn't look like soldiers at all, despite the uniforms, the guns, the ugly green truck they rode in along the Metropolitan Expressway. That was during a time I didn't understand very well, except that I was scared and angry, and for a while I wanted to see Montreal filled with soldiers. Let them come from everywhere in the country to protect us.

And when I hear the theme to *Elvira Madigan*, I think of a photograph on the TV news, of a Quebec politician I'd never seen before, and films of a black car with a gaping trunk.

There were terrorists in Montreal then, and sometimes the news would report that a bomb had exploded downtown, usually in a mailbox. After one of those reports when I was about twelve I was afraid to go downtown. My mother told me I was being silly. "It's not going to happen," she said with so much certainty that I believed her, although I couldn't see why I should. Yet it did seem that bombs went off in places I would never go; they certainly wouldn't explode in Côte-des-Neiges District, or Ville St. Laurent, or Ste. Catherine Street where everybody shopped downtown. Terrorists attacked vaguely unrespectable or alien areas of the city: near the harbour, or on the French side across St. Lawrence Blvd.

On "Pulse News" the reporters interviewed policemen who assured everyone that the separatist terrorists would be captured. My Dad watched those reports leaning toward the TV, hands folded tightly between his knees. "Sons of bitches," he said.

"Hank," my mother said warningly.

"He hears worse at school." I did. By now I was going to Gardenview, where the kids swore freely—far worse than back at Bedford. I had tried to resist, but I started to use those words myself, just to keep up with the other kids, but only at school, of course. "People are going to get killed like this." Dad was talking about innocent people, regular people who weren't policemen. It was different with those who wore uniforms.

"There's always some of the Fransoys who are trouble-makers," my mother commented, and I remembered the stories she'd told me about French gangs who got into fights with the Jewish ones back in her old neighbourhood. I pictured pitched battles in the streets, although I couldn't imagine how the two sides were able to tell each other apart once they melded together in a wild fistfight. I knew it wouldn't be like the fights in Westerns, where you always knew who were the good guys and who were the bad guys.

How could you be sure *what* the terrorists wouldn't bomb? What made the terrorists most frightening was that you had no idea who or where they were, or what they'd do. They weren't in uniforms, they weren't grouped together across a battlefield; they lurked in normal houses, planning horrors you could never foresee.

* * *

Dad subscribed to the *Chicago Sun-Times* Sunday paper, because his parents lived in Chicago and that was how he kept up with what was happening to their city and country. As long as the Russians were a threat to everyone, we and the Americans were bound to be on the same side, and since I watched so much American TV I thought we were pretty much the same anyway. I only saw my "other" grandparents during family events—weddings, Bar Mitzvahs, funerals—so I didn't know them very well. But they were a source of mystery and pride for me; I not only knew but was related to real Americans, the people who counted in the world.

One Sunday, the picture magazine that came with the paper had a report on "wargaming." Grown men in the States got together and staged battles on table tops involving soldiers smaller than my own, but in staggering numbers. According to the article, hundreds of soldiers, tanks, and cannon were deployed on both sides. By then, I had mostly outgrown my soldiers, at least in the sense of wanting to crawl around the floor throwing bricks at them. But the article said that wargaming involved elaborate rules using rulers and dice to govern movement and determine casualties. It seemed fairly simple to recreate what the article was describing. Rules would make my own battles more fair and sensible, even if there was a risk the wrong side would win. To my knowledge, the good guys always won; if they didn't, Hitler would have conquered Europe, the Germans would have won World War I, the British would have crushed the Americans back in 1776 and democracy would have suffered. Still, at thirteen I was ready for a better way to handle my wars, so I designed a set of complicated rules and tried them out in my room. My battles took longer, but were all the more satisfying for it, because they seemed more real.

My best friend at the time was Paul Schneider, and one

of the things we shared was that we were good at history. We could talk sometimes about battles; I was more interested in World War II, while he preferred the older periods, like the American Revolution and the War of 1812. He had a collection of small blue and red soldiers from the Revolutionary War, which he'd bought from an ad on the back of a comic book. He'd also ordered a set of ancient Romans, but they were breakable and few of them remained intact.

I told him at recess one day about the wargaming rules, and asked him: "You want to try them with our troops?"

"Sure. Yours are bigger than mine, though."

"We'll figure out what to do."

"Where do you want to do it? I don't know if we can use my dining room table." That was the biggest table I'd ever seen. But his mother was very protective of it, and refused to allow us to do school projects together on it unless we covered it with layers of newspaper. Carpets made both our living-room floors tough to manoeuvre troops around.

The best floors were in my room and down in our basement. My bedroom was too small for a full-scale battle — there was very little free surface, especially when I had school stuff scattered around. My Dad used the basement for his office, but I thought there was a chance since tax season was over at last and his business was light these days. And school was coming to an end, meaning that the bigger projects of the year were done, so I could take off a Saturday afternoon without worrying about lots of homework.

We planned our battle for a Saturday when my parents were going to be out of the house anyway; my Uncle Joe was in the Jewish General, and my parents were going to visit him. Uncle Joe was one of an uncountable number of uncles and aunts my mother had, and I was never able to get them entirely straight in my mind, although I knew Uncle Joe to be the one with the gruff voice and the violent opinions.

Of course, I cleared everything with my parents first. I thought I'd managed to explain the plan to my mother, but then on that Saturday she asked: "*What* are you going to do?"

"A wargame."

"You're going to make a mess, that's what," she said as she pulled on her spring jacket. "Clean up before we come home."

My father was trying to gather his stuff together: wallet, keys, a small pad and pen so that he could write down whatever the doctors said. But he took a moment to say: "Keep out of the office, eh, Lar? I don't want you mixing up the papers."

"I won't." The sounds of the Fifth Dimension thumped from my sister's room. Sheila had rolled her eyes with extra drama at what Paul and I were planning to do, declaring it "so babyish." I actually couldn't completely disagree with that; part of me wondered if at thirteen I ought to be doing anything at all with my toy soldiers, no matter how sophisticated the rules. But men wargamed, and made sure their games were historically accurate. Anyway, I would be going to high school in the fall. This was my last chance to act like a kid before I entered a frightening world of teenagers who dated, drove cars, and took drugs—if what I saw of high school on TV was to be believed. I simply refused to let myself be embarrassed.

"Have a good time," my mother said as she pulled open

the front door. "And be sure it's all cleaned up by the time we get home. I'll tell your Uncle Joe you said hi."

"Okay." I watched her exit into the soft May air. Montreal springs were long; you could savour the temperature gradually rising day by day till the middle of June. I probably should have been doing something outside — so many times during summers, my mother would come into the living room to see me watching TV and say: "Why aren't you playing outside?" "Playing" — was I still expected to do that? Or were you supposed to use a different word after thirteen?

As soon as my parents were gone I went into the basement and mentally declared it my own. Thanks to Dad's business, I didn't get to use it very much; now, I had the whole, wide tiled floor, from the bottom of the staircase to the bar we never used, and even beyond to the area opposite the office door. The basement was in an L-shape, and the bottom of the L was where we'd put our old TV, and a tattered chesterfield for Dad's clients to sit on while waiting for him.

I got out my soldiers and divided them into their two armies, designating a starting point for each that would give them plenty of room to manoeuvre. I didn't bother standing them all up, just enough to get started. My rules governed movement and firepower for both infantry and the diverse collection of armoured vehicles I could muster. Each side would get its share of "tanks" (some of them really cowboy wagons and Dinky cars pressed into service) that could move twice as fast as infantry and inflict twice as many casualties with one volley. A volley was a roll of the two dice I'd borrowed from our Monopoly game. Paul would supply the artillery, even if the cannon were tiny contributions from his Revolutionary War set that were nowhere near to scale with my infantry. We would have to make all sorts of allowances, pretending, for example, that tomahawk-wielding Indians were simply stand-ins for World War II soldiers. For measuring movement, I had a yardstick from Gotlieb's Apparel, one of my Dad's clients.

Paul arrived a bit late, a small suitcase in his hand. "I had to help with the order," he said. Like my own mother, Mrs. Schneider shopped at Esposito's in the St. Louis Shopping Centre; and like me, he was expected to put away the order once it was delivered.

"That's okay. What did you bring?"

"Come on." We went downstairs and he looked at the troops awaiting battle. "Jeez, how many do you have altogether, anyways?"

"A hundred and twelve." I'd even once made a chart of all my holdings, divided into categories. One of the best sets was made up of soldiers I'd gotten from cereal boxes—a series of Soldiers of All Times, including two musketeers, a Foreign Legionnaire, and a Swiss archer, moulded in dark gold plastic. I was thoroughly proud of my collection.

"I just have sixty." He brought out his Revolutionary soldiers plus some World War I soldiers who were halfway in size between the Revolutionaries and my own. "But I brought some cannon, too." He had artillery that would fit a lot better than the little ones we were originally planning to use. "My mother was going to throw all this out but I wouldn't let her."

"How could she throw out something that's yours?" I wouldn't let my mother come anywhere near my stuff.

"She said it was just junk. I wasn't playing with them much any more." He looked around the floor. "Is this the battlefield? I hope it's big enough."

"It's all we've got."

"Yeah."

My sister had switched to the Rolling Stones. I thought something martial would make more sense; I'd seen the movie *The Longest Day* not too long before, and thought it would be great to have some music like that.

"We could use your World War I's," I said, "but it'll be tough doing the movements with those little ones."

"Might as well try. It'll work."

I was doubtful, but as far as I was concerned a battle needed as many soldiers as possible to make it proper. And spectacular—while Paul added his soldiers to the two armies, I went upstairs to get my parents' Swinger camera. I wanted to record the sight of soldiers filling the basement: hordes of troops pounding each other in an epic battle.

* * *

The army I saw that October was the Canadian army. I knew we had an army of our own, of course, but I always found the idea strange; the TV shows, the movies, the comic books, and just about everything else showed only the Americans as the ones fighting and beating the Germans and Japanese, so I couldn't help thinking of them as "our" army. Also, armies fought in other places: Asian jungles and European cities, where they mowed down enemy soldiers by the dozens. If we had an army, it should be overseas somewhere, facing down the Communists.

Dealing with criminals at home was the job of the police. Those tall, heavy-set men with moustaches, like the ones who sometimes visited my schools to talk about safety on the roads, must have had incredible, borderline magical techniques for investigating crimes. After all, they did nothing else the whole day.

So when James Cross was kidnapped, I figured the police would track his kidnappers down and free him in a matter of days. For a while, the news was too crazy to believe: members of the F.L.Q. had snatched Cross and hidden him away somewhere in Montreal. My father had always watched the news intently, mainly to see if we were going to face World War III with the Russians over Vietnam. But now he wouldn't let us talk to him, and he wouldn't eat supper or go to bed, till he'd absorbed all the reports on the different channels. Even the American channels, the ones in Plattsburgh and Burlington, reported on the kidnapping.

"Hank, it's the same story over and over," my mother said to him as he got up to switch back and forth between channels. I could see he was probably wearing out the tuner as he spun the clacking knob around and around.

"Yeah," Dad said, not really listening to her. "Shh! What's this?"

Then there'd be another report, one that may have meant absolutely nothing, but Dad couldn't tear himself away. Only when some story about Trudeau or the economy came on did he walk over to the TV and close it with a smack. "Separatist bastards."

Separatist: The word made you freeze with horror, like "Communist" and "gangster." I knew separatists wanted to destroy Canada, and make us all French. The majority of

French-Canadians didn't agree with them—the separatist party had lost the election badly that year—but there was no knowing exactly how many separatists there were, how many of them thought kidnapping people was okay.

I had my own problems then: coping with a new way of going to school. Every subject in a different room with a different teacher; kids who were mostly older, bigger, far more grown up than I'd ever be. Some of the guys even had beards. My high school had a lounge downstairs where the kids who never went to class hung out; it stank of cigarettes, both regular and marijuana, and the carpet and cloth-covered benches were speckled with burn marks. Gym meant showers; Chemistry involved sitting in a lab surrounded by bottles with unidentifiable but clearly dangerous, maybe explosive, liquids in them; French was taught by a boring guy with an unplaceable accent, in a room with stale, oft-breathed air. If it weren't for World History and English Lit, I was sure I would drown in it all. And I was one of the smallest kids in the school—easy to push around, even beat up, if I wasn't careful.

And now all this.

Five days after James Cross was kidnapped, the separatists struck again: Pierre Laporte was kidnapped right outside his house. And he lived in St. Lambert, which sounded far too much like St. Laurent, our own suburb. The two weren't actually close to one another, but now even my sister, who seldom cared about the news, was getting worried. "What's going *on*?" she asked as she watched the "Pulse" reporter talking into the camera set up outside Laporte's home.

They were everywhere. You never knew where they

would strike. I had a load of homework to do after supper, but I knew I wouldn't be able to think about Chapter 3 of *Lord of the Flies*. This was becoming too much, and I wanted the rest of Canada to send all its policemen to Montreal, to put aside whatever stupid little crimes they were trying to investigate and come where the real trouble was, where people were being grabbed out of their own houses and taken down into dark places where they couldn't be found.

The morning after Thanksgiving, my mother knocked on my bedroom door to wake me up, but her knock was more abrupt than usual. When I opened my bedroom door I heard CJAD blaring from the old, hissing kitchen radio. Sheila was already awake and poking her head out her own door.

"What's going on?" she asked me.

"I don't know."

My mother came back down the hall to make sure we were awake for school. She saw us and stopped cold, and I realized we must have looked like scared little animals peeking out from their burrows.

"Ma?" I asked. "What—?"

"They called out the army," she said. "They're all over Ottawa, protecting the government."

* * *

When Paul and I laid out our troops, I naturally chose to be the Americans, giving him the Allies. He had no objection to that, and even seemed to like the idea that his "divisions," as I called them, were so different from one another. He could give the World War I's and the Russians and the

Indians very different missions, while my more uniform army was like a huge horde trying to swamp the other side.

We marched our troops toward each other, applying my movement rules even though it seemed to take forever for the two armies to come within range. I knew that no weapon could be very effective at any great distance, so I made up a rule that the soldiers could only start firing when they got to within one foot of the enemy. We spent a good half-hour just marching.

"This is boring," Paul said. "Couldn't we speed them up?"

"We have to stay in the rules or there's no point having them."

"I know. They were even slower in Napoleon's day."

I had too many soldiers for the size of the battlefield; the columns of troops kept threatening to march into each other. I moved my tanks to the sides to give them room, and Paul was busily doing the same thing. I wasn't sure what to do with my artillery. Should I put them with the infantry or in a position to blast Paul's tanks?

When the two sides finally met, we faced our first problem. When I wargamed by myself, I had the two armies take turns shooting at each other, so one side (usually the Allies) ended up at a distinct disadvantage since they didn't fire till they'd suffered casualties and had fewer shooters. But Paul and I had to fire simultaneously, and so we had to come up with rules about when casualties from artillery, tanks, and infantry fire would be calculated and removed.

"This is getting crazy," Paul said as I rolled the dice. We were doing far more math than fighting.

"What else can we do?" He couldn't seem to understand that it all had to be this way, if the battle was going to be proper. He was liking my rules less and less, and I wondered if he wouldn't prefer to just wing Lego bricks at the soldiers after all. I was starting to get tired of adding and dividing, too. I wondered if it wouldn't have been better to forget the rules and become as babyish as my sister thought we were anyway. "It'll be okay," I said. I took a couple more pictures, anxious to record the sight of all those soldiers covering the basement floor. I knew I'd never have another battle like it.

I desperately wanted to win, but as time went on strange things were happening—the battle was going *both* ways. On the left side, I was doing pretty well, and was busily slaughtering his Russians and Revolutionary British. But on the right side I was in serious trouble. I turned some of my artillery on his advancing Indians.

"Hey! No fair!"

"What?"

"You can't just move your cannons like that!"

"I'm just re-aiming them."

"Then you have to leave time to do that. You can't just move them and then get all the same firepower."

"Why not?"

We argued about it for far too long, till finally I recognized that if we didn't get back to shooting at each other we'd never get the game finished. I reluctantly conceded that my cannons would only be awarded half their usual casualties, to account for the time taken in re-positioning them. Paul wasn't entirely happy, but at least we were back to rolling the dice and removing the killed. We had no rules for woundeds, because there seemed no point. Removal from the battlefield was all that counted. We argued over rules governing bazooka-men. Should they count as artillery? For just one volley? Every time I thought we were moving along well, Paul would come up with another complication, till I got fed up.

I got some good dice rolls, especially on the left, and he sent in reinforcements. But on the right I was losing badly, and I could see that whole side starting to collapse. We'd end up turning our armies ninety degrees, which made no sense at all.

Worse than that, the game was taking far longer than I'd imagined. We both still had enough soldiers to keep going for hours — but my parents would be home soon. My sister was now watching TV upstairs, and I could hear the Canadian rock-music show she liked, the one that copied *American Bandstand*.

I had to go to the bathroom, and when I came back I looked at the battlefield in dismay. It was a mess. Our positions were twisted around, and divisions remained in what seemed like permanent reserve, since there wasn't enough space on the floor to bring them into action.

"I've got to get home soon," Paul said. For a second I thought he was being a terrible traitor to the game, but I understood. I had to get the battle wrapped up, and the soldiers put away, before too long. We might keep on blasting each other for another hour or so, but that wouldn't settle anything.

"Yeah," I said. "Sure."

* * *

All the horrors of that October seemed to happen while I was asleep, and I would wake up to find there'd been another decision, another move. A few days after the army took up positions in Ottawa, I woke up to learn that the War Measures Act had been invoked.

"What does *that* mean?" I asked Dad.

"It's like we're in a war now," he said. We sat at breakfast, my father wearing his frayed robe that bunched around the shoulders as he leaned toward the radio. It was as if we'd become like the United States, with its protests and its race riots, only worse. My father jerked suddenly. "No! Not like in a war, not like that."

"Why not?" I found it hard to believe him now, no matter how he tried to take back his words. *Why not?*

"They're sending in the army to find Cross and Laporte. To arrest all those people helping the terrorists."

"Good." *Good*! I thought. Send in the army. Fill the streets with them. Catch the separatists. In my mind I cheered on Trudeau, thanked him for doing it at last.

"Is there still school?" Sheila asked. "What are we supposed to do?"

"Oh, yeah. Go ahead," Dad said. "It's all downtown anyways."

We were supposed to behave like normal. I knew that was ridiculous. I went to school that day, and the teachers focused on their subjects — all except our World History teacher, who tried to explain to us about the War Measures Act, how this was the first time it had been invoked when there wasn't actually a war. Since it was high school, and she didn't know how to control a class, most of the kids didn't pay much attention. I listened, but it all seemed unreal. The army was downtown: twenty minutes away from our old neighbourhood by train. Hundreds or even thousands of terrorists were out there somewhere. There was no telling what they'd do next.

I came home from school to find my parents in the basement office working with a client. The TV was mercifully closed, its charcoal-gray screen empty and silent. I did my homework; there was so much of it now that I was in high school, and I didn't mind, because doing Math problems seemed refreshingly *normal*. For an hour, I could pretend nothing else was going on.

Later, though, the TV came back on, and we ate supper in the living room, watching the news as we balanced our plates on the fragile TV trays. The camera showed downtown shots: soldiers in helmets, carrying rifles, standing on corners outside banks and stores. I loved seeing them. We were safe now, I thought, no matter what would happen.

* * *

Paul and I kept up the game for a little while longer, firing and trying to manoeuvre into new positions without having enough room to do it. But it was obvious that we wouldn't finish the game in time. My parents would be home any minute, and they'd kill me if the basement were still like this.

"We're going to have to stop," I said.

"Yeah."

Paul let out a violent sigh. I watched him gather up his soldiers and cannon and scoop them into his small suitcase. "That was great," he said, but I could tell he didn't mean it. He looked tired, as if my rules had ruined the game or it had gone on much longer than he'd wanted. I was afraid that

I'd drawn him into a dull, draining waste of time, that he'd never want to play again. I wasn't sure I wanted to, either. I returned my soldiers to their plastic bags, mixing up the dead and the living until all our calculations were completely wiped out. Soon, the basement looked normal again.

As he was leaving, Paul said: "We needed to get the rules better organized, that's all."

"Yeah." But I'd done my best; what more did he expect?

"See you." I noticed he didn't say we ought to try again sometime.

Back in my room, I stashed my soldiers in their cardboard box in the closet. I heard the front door grunt open, and my parents talking. I was pretty sure I'd done a good job cleaning up the basement, and wouldn't get into trouble. Still, over the next few days I'd find the occasional soldier under the radiator or chesterfield.

* * *

The day after the imposition of the War Measures Act, I couldn't believe that the schools were still open, and that everything was going on as if nothing were wrong. We were at war—no matter what my father tried to say—and yet we did World History and French and Math like always. After school, I went to the variety store to buy some "Man on the Moon" cards. Just as I turned the corner onto Alexis Nihon Boulevard, I heard a strange rumbling coming from the Metropolitan Expressway, which passed not far beyond the end of the street. I caught a glimpse of a green truck, and the swaying helmeted heads of the soldiers sitting in its open box, just before it disappeared behind one of the tall apartment buildings that lined the highway. I couldn't see them as anything but men in ridiculous-looking clothes, completely *wrong* among the tractor-trailers and cars that slid by.

At lunch, I found Paul in the caf. I was still sort-of friends with him, but things were never the same after our wargame. I told him what I'd seen. "Seriously?" he said, eyes widening. "Jeez." We didn't talk about the game; as it turned out, we would never wargame again, although in the weeks till school ended we would still talk about armies, battles, tactics. "My mother says they'll catch those separatists soon."

"Probably," I said. "I hope so." It wasn't just because I wanted the separatists stopped. I didn't want to see the soldiers again, even on TV.

That night they announced that Pierre Laporte had been found dead in the trunk of a car. We could see the rear of the black car, but no body. Then CFCF showed a photograph of Laporte, and played a sombre classical tune. My father made the "*Tz*" sound over and over again; my mother kept her hand clamped over her mouth; my sister was utterly silent. I'll never forget how badly I wanted the picture to go away, the music to stop.

Enemies

WHILE I WAS growing up, the world was divided neatly into halves. I would never have believed that one day the Soviet Union and Warsaw Pact would just vanish, without a world war, and suddenly we'd no longer be facing hateful enemies big enough to destroy us. By "us" I meant mainly Canada and the United States. I grew up watching American TV, reading their books, listening to their music, like every other Canadian, and when I was very small I even thought we were somehow one country.

The biggest enemy, of course, was Russia, which opposed everything right: free speech, elections, freedom for the Jews to practise their religion or emigrate to Israel, even the truth. The Russians lied to their own people, including children, who were subjected to shocking brainwashing from the minute they entered school. I found nothing more horrible about the Russians than the way they lied to kids, raising them to believe complete nonsense, like how wonderful Stalin was.

I understood the Russians better than most people. My father was Hungarian, or at least his parents were, and most of his friends and bookkeeping clients had escaped from Hungary after the war or during the Revolution in 1956. I heard stories from them and my "other" grandparents, Zaidy and Bubby Teitel, who now lived in Chicago, about the Germans and the Russians, about horrors, atrocities. During the war the Russians were our sort-of friends, but only because they were against the Germans, too. The Russians "liberated" Hungary, meaning they kicked the Germans out so they could control the country themselves; the very word "liberation" was a lie, a sick joke. Now, the Germans were our friends, mainly because they were against the Russians. Once Hitler was gone, the Germans were okay. But they'd let him get away with his crimes against the Jews and even helped him. Maybe some had had no choice, but others could have refused. There was no excuse, especially "I was just following orders."

I knew about our enemies mostly because of my Aunt Ellen, who'd barely survived in the Budapest ghetto during the war. She and my grandparents were all the family I had on my father's side. Zaidy and Bubby Teitel left Europe before the war, smart enough to see what was happening before things got too bad. But Aunt Ellen had stayed behind, risking everything. From the little my father told me, I understood that she'd been very lucky; the Russians got to the ghetto before the Germans could kill the rest of the Jews. Aunt Ellen spoke virtually no English, so I couldn't ask her anything directly, and she didn't tell my father much about what she'd gone through.

One of my father's clients, Mr. Koltai, told me stories about the Russians stealing everything, the Stalinists who were brought in to take over, Russian tanks in the streets of Budapest in 1956. We sometimes sat together on the basement chesterfield as he waited for my father, and when I had a message to pass on to Dad from my mother. I thought it was ridiculous that I had to wait there for him like one of his bookkeeping customers.

"I hate the Russians," I told Mr. Koltai, who looked down at me but didn't nod as I'd expected him to. It was all I knew to say. I hated them and wished I could slaughter them.

* * *

That's why I was stunned to learn that one of my best friends in high school was Russian. I met Sammy Borodin during my second year at Sir Winston Churchill High. Everything in high school was still confusing. In the beginning I'd been overwhelmed by having to pick my own courses—compulsory, non-compulsory, interest—and going from class to class, teacher to teacher, all over the building. My voice had changed, I was getting pimples, all around me kids were wearing their hair longer than ever, and the smell of cigarette smoke and even pot came from the student "lounge" down in the basement near the Woodworking and Metalwork shops. I thought things would become clearer by the time I reached Grade 9, but there were still confusions and complications. I mistakenly took a course for the second time, because its name had changed over the summer. I had a locker with a warped latch that would barely accept my combination lock; once, not long after the Christmas break, I left the lock open, and someone stole my new math set. My books and winter coat were still there; only the little tin box with its clear plastic protractor, ruler, and squares, the metal compass and divider, was gone. Sammy had the locker next to mine, and he was putting away his Tech Drawing textbook when he saw me slam the locker door in fury. I knew him as just another kid in my homeroom and some other classes, though he wasn't in Enriched English.

"What's the matter?" he asked.

I told him. "That cost me three dollars!" I said; my parents had paid for it, but that wasn't the point; in fact, it made me even more responsible. It wasn't the cost—not entirely —it was that someone had grabbed *my* property. If I'd seen an open locker somewhere I never would have gone into it and started taking things. "Bastard," I said.

"Want to borrow mine?"

"No, that's okay. Thanks anyway."

"You're Lawrence, right?"

"Yeah. Sammy?" He nodded and we shook hands.

"We should find the fucker."

"How?"

"I don't know." He thought for a moment. "Leave the locker open again. Watch for whoever goes for it. Trap him and beat his head in."

It sounded like a good idea. But I knew it would be a waste of time. "Never mind."

Sammy shrugged. "Okay."

We were in the same Intro to Physical Science class so we both walked upstairs to the lab. It felt safer having someone to walk around with. Now that I was one of the smallest kids again—after finally becoming one of the "big kids" in elementary school—school was a more dangerous, an alien place. There were kids six feet tall, with blank eyes, who seemed ready to kill anybody who looked at them wrong; girls with huge breasts that made them seem far too old to be in the same school as me; and a whole crowd of kids who hung out in the lounge and never went to any class except shop. They were the scariest of all. Who knew what they'd do while on drugs? They were as unpredictable, mindlessly violent, filled with bizarre ideas as the Russians.

"What do you think of Mrs. Young?" he asked. She was our homeroom teacher and taught Canadian History. I wasn't sure what to say; the wrong answer made you look like a fool—I'd learned that much at high school. Two kids were making out in the stairwell, their streaked jeans tangled together.

I said: "She's okay. Boring, though."

"Yeah, boring all right. She sounds like *she's* bored."

"I know." She spoke in a monotone. "She's probably taught this stuff a thousand times already."

"At least she knows what she's talking about. Ever have Mr. Holik for Math?"

"Yeah, this year." Mr. Holik was always correcting himself. He'd once filled a blackboard with equations, trying to get to the zero he knew should be at the end, only to realize he'd messed up at the very beginning. "He's the worst Math teacher I ever had." My elementary-school teachers had been much better.

"I had him last year. He stinks. You play chess?"

"Yeah. Not well." I'd thought about taking Chess, one of the non-credit interest courses, along with other bird courses like Film and Computer Science, but couldn't face the prospect of being beaten all the time. My father had taught me to play, then proceeded to slaughter me in every game.

"Doesn't matter. I hang out at the Chess Club. Come on after school. Play with Gordy Baltovitch—he stinks. You'll beat him for sure."

Most of the kids I knew at Sir Winnie belonged to things that seemed intimidating or sissy or both: Band, the *Reach for the Top* team. I'd tried out for one of the floor hockey teams but was too little. Floor hockey was actually ringuette, which we Jewish kids called "bagel hockey," and in Phys Ed I had trouble stickhandling the bagel using those overlong poles. The Chess Club seemed more my speed. No matter how bad I was, at least I wouldn't be humiliated in front of all that many guys.

"Okay, sure."

After school, I met him outside the lounge. In a cramped room nearby, a bunch of kids hung around—all boys except for one girl who rolled her eyes at the boob jokes—some of them playing chess but most of them talking: about hockey, music, teachers. The chess they played was the timed variety, not the long games my father used to play with me or his friends on Sunday afternoons. Double-faced clocks ticked beside the boards. A guy wouldn't just slide his piece into a captured piece's square, then slowly remove the prisoner; he'd grab his opponent's man in his fist as he plonked down his own before the square got cold. After each move he smacked down the button to stop his clock and start his opponent's going again. A transistor radio tuned to CKGM blared in the corner, and a hard-rock group I didn't know screamed away.

"Hey," Sammy announced, "here's a new victim."

"You play?" one of the guys asked. It seemed like a stupid question, but maybe some people came to learn, or just hang out.

"Yeah, kind of."

Sammy made the introductions. Steven Yakibchuk and Jerry Kalter beat me handily at games I couldn't get out of. Since I expected to lose it didn't bother me too much; it was fun exchanging dirty jokes or evaluations of the teachers with the others. I kept looking at the girl, Janie Kalypopolous, but she avoided making eye contact, and I was struck by how easily she kibbitzed and swore with the others. Then I played Gordy Baltovitch and creamed him in fewer than twenty moves.

Sammy and I played one game, and it went on for quite a long time; we were down to rooks and pawns, but he had more pawns and I couldn't stop him from promoting one to a queen.

"Good game," he said, and held out his hand.

"Thanks." I hoped I'd be that polite if I ever won.

* * *

He was better than I was, but sometimes too fast for his own good, and lost rooks and even his queen to me because he didn't pay attention to my threats. I started to learn openings from the others, and how to avoid the stupid Crazy Queen opening when she ran around grabbing pieces all over the board. There were seven members of the Club, but only Steven, Jerry, and Sammy came all the time. Mr. Sandor —the Woodworking teacher who also offered the Chess course—showed up once in a while because he was the club's "staff advisor." I still sometimes saw my other friends, guys I'd known in elementary school, like Paul Schneider, or those I knew well enough at Sir Winnie to share a lunch table with in the cafeteria.

Sammy and I had lots in common besides chess. We were both interested in the space program, and had sisters who drove us crazy. I enjoyed hearing him voice the feelings I shared about teachers, girls (they still scared me too much to talk to them), TV shows. He liked science fiction, too, and we could discuss the relative merits of *Land of the Giants* and the old *Star Trek* series, which the CBC channel ran on Saturday afternoons.

"That was a great show," Sammy said. I still remembered *Lost in Space* fondly, but had to admit *Star Trek* was better. "Sometimes Kirk was stupid, but those aliens were great." He'd built a model Enterprise with nacelles that lit up. He showed it to me when I visited his house the first time, on the other side of Côte Vertu.

I twisted the orange-tinted nacelle noses to make the little light-bulbs glow. The Jupiter II was a passive ship, subject to whatever outer space or aliens threw at it. The Enterprise could fight back. "Its design is cool," I said; it wasn't like other spaceships, which were all rockets or saucers.

"Yeah. Look at this." He pulled out a project he was doing in Tech Drawing: he'd made a schema of a space station, with cutaways and perspective. "I found the design in a NASA book."

By now, the Apollo flights were happening twice a year or so, and men—American men—were going to the moon without trouble, except for Apollo 13. And even then, they'd managed to fix the problem. The Space Race was over; at least that was one area where the fight was finished, and the good guys had definitely won. "Cool, eh?" Sammy said. It was.

As I was leaving I saw a picture hanging on the wall just inside the front door. I knew it as a Madonna; there was Mary holding a little Jesus. Mary's gold halo was real metal, not just paint. "Oh," I said.

"What?"

"Nothing."

For some reason I'd assumed Sammy was Jewish. The fact that he was Christian didn't bother me too much. He wasn't my first non-Jewish friend; I'd been friends with a French-Canadian kid back in Grade 4. But I still worried about being a good Jew, and watched out for Christians trying to push their religion on me, like the Jehovah's Witnesses who showed up at our door despite the fact it was a Jewish neighbourhood. I couldn't get it out of my head that Christians had been responsible for most of the Jews' troubles over history, until the Arabs took over. My mother told me the Popes had even encouraged anti-Semitism, and that's why so many French-Canadians hated Jews. Sammy seemed all right, but he was different and that could mean anything.

"It's an icon."

"Yeah?"

"Yeah. It was my grandmother's. Maybe even older."

"So you're what? Catholic?"

"No, Russian Orthodox."

Russian? I was stunned. And "orthodox"? I couldn't make

sense of what he'd said. "Orthodox" what? I knew what Orthodox Judaism meant. But how could you just be "orthodox"?

"What?" he asked, annoyed and defensive.

"I was just wondering." If he was an orthodox Christian he couldn't have been a Communist, who were all atheists. But he was still Russian.

"Okay then."

"Okay. See you."

As I walked home I thought of Aunt Ellen, and all she'd been through. At supper that night, I asked Dad why Aunt Ellen didn't leave Hungary with Bubby and Zaidy Teitel.

"She wanted to stay behind," he said around a mouthful of beef stew. My mother wasn't listening; she focused on the "Women's" section of the *Star*. I was afraid she'd try to stop me from bringing unpleasant subjects to the dinner table. My sister had stopped eating by now and was listening, too. "No matter how hard they tried she wouldn't go."

"How come?" I couldn't believe she'd be that stupid.

"She couldn't just leave the place," my father said, wiping his mouth. "It was her home." He made an odd sound. "Who needs it?" I saw him glare at a spot on the table, as if it was crawling with bugs. I'd never seen him so angry, except when my sister or I were little and had done something seriously wrong.

"Hank," my mother said warningly, I'm not sure about what.

"*Animals*," my father said so sharply I nearly jumped, then he went back to his stew.

Later, we sat on our front porch watching the planes roar past on their way into Dorval. They flew so close we could read the logos as easily as if they were on TV. Dad held a cigar, and took a puff whenever a plane went over and there was no point in trying to talk anyway. My mother was inside checking invoices for my father; she was spending a lot of time on his bookkeeping business, and I hardly ever talked to her any more. Sheila was at her own club at school: She was doing drama, rehearsing *Fiddler on the Roof.*

"I still don't get why Aunt Ellen wanted to stay there."

"I told you. It was her home." A plane flew over, and he sucked on the cigar. Blue-gray smoke swirled around the porchlight. When he could be heard again, he said: "God-damn Hungarians."

"What? We're Hungarians."

"Not them, no. We aren't them."

I knew what he meant: because we were Jews more than Hungarians. During the war Hungary had reluctantly been on the German side, but they'd formed the Arrow Cross, so they weren't so innocent after all. Still, they'd mostly want-ed Hitler to leave them alone … and now they were the enemies again, on the side of the Russians. But—just like before—not by choice; they were being forced into it, they had Russian guns to their heads. I knew that well enough. If there was a war—and it was pretty clear there'd be one —they'd fight on the Russian side and we'd have to kill them. So whose side were they really on?

"How is Aunt Ellen related to us again?" He'd told me a couple of times before, but I always forgot.

"Ellenin—your Aunt Ellen and your Bubby Teitel are half-sisters. Your great-grandfather Emil married twice; they're his daughters by different wives."

"How come she doesn't talk about what happened to her there?"

"She doesn't like to talk about it. Most of them don't. Why dirty up other people with that sh—" I couldn't believe what he'd almost said; I'd never heard him use that word before. He'd changed so much since he started that business. "Anyway, what's past is past." But I knew he didn't believe that. Not the way he'd always talked about Hitler, or the Russians.

"You mean she loved Hungary so much she was ready to die to stay there?" That was crazy.

Dad shrugged. "She didn't know what was going to happen. Nobody did." We had to wait for another plane to go over: K.L.M. He took another puff of his cigar; he only smoked during hockey games and when it warm enough to sit outside at night. Nowadays, he seldom had the time. "It's easy to say that now. She didn't know the future any more than we do. You don't expect your neighbours to turn on you like that."

Animals. Your own people suddenly became your enemies. You never knew who you could trust.

We could see the lights of the next plane in the distance, two glimmering red specks vastly different from the stars and planets I sometimes tried to spot. "After the war, she had nobody, nothing. So your grandparents got her out of there, finally. She was one of the last to leave."

"Really?"

"Yeah. They came to Montreal, then when my father moved to Chicago she stayed put. She didn't feel like moving again."

"So what do you think of Russians?" I wanted to know what he'd think of my having Sammy as a friend, though I was sure he wouldn't care. I shouldn't, either, but I couldn't help thinking about it.

"Let them get out of Hungary," he said, stabbing the darkness with his cigar. I'd never seen him, heard him, like this. "Let them leave Israel alone, stop sending weapons to the Arabs. Let's see them let the Jews out. Then ask me about those goddamn Russians." He picked something out of his teeth with the same hand that clutched the cigar, and said nothing more, even though it was long before the next plane became too loud.

* * *

From then on, I wanted to win those chess games with Sammy more than ever. This wasn't just about us any more. I felt I'd failed Canada, or maybe Hungary, every time I lost to him, and I when I beat him I was showing that we could play, too.

And I tested him, silently. I watched for his opinions, his preferences. Part of me knew I was being ridiculous, but I couldn't help measuring the things he said, to see who he really was and where he stood. The Vietnam War was still going on, and every night the reports came in about how many enemy soldiers and how many Americans had died. The number for the North Vietnamese and the Viet Cong were always higher, so I figured it was inevitable that the Americans would win. It was always sad to hear about those dozens of "good guy" deaths, just as you hated to see cavalrymen get shot with arrows in Westerns or Americans and British soldiers die in movies like *The Longest Day*. But at least the Americans were winning.

I asked Sammy about Vietnam during one of our games. I was supposed to be concentrating on the board and the clock, but instead I asked him what he thought was going to happen.

"I don't know. Here!" He grabbed one of my knights, and in return I took his bishop. An even trade, if you went purely by points, although I found bishops better because you could see what they were capable of doing, or where they threatened to go, more easily. Knights were devious, creating forks when you least expected it. You couldn't block them, and sometimes their "L" movements were hard to visualize. "It's a fucking stupid war."

"Why?"

He moved up a pawn; he liked to form long stepped formations of pawns. Grab the lowermost one, and the whole structure collapsed, but it was always hidden behind a solid wall. "What good are they doing there?"

"Stopping the Communists." I knew all about the Domino Effect. Cambodia, Laos, eventually Thailand and who knew what else: They'd all fall. "You have to stop them or they'll take over." I threatened his key pawn with one of the two rooks I'd lined up side-by-side in the middle of my first rank. I knew he'd counter with a distant, impossible-to-chase-away knight.

"You can't win in Vietnam. It's all jungle!"

"So what?"

"So they hide in the tunnels when you bomb them then come out and kill you. Yeah!" He thrust a bishop attack at me on the other side; I waited for him to extend his forces too far, as he sometimes did. "That's what I'd do. That's what they're doing."

"But they're getting slaughtered."

"They got more where those came from. They don't care about human life. They send thousands out there to be killed and find thousands more till there are no more Americans left. They're crazy." His queen was stuck behind a couple of pawns, but he didn't seem anxious to break up his formation to let her free to help the bishop. As soon as he did ... I kept pressing against his bishop till he had no choice. Then I began snapping up pawns while he went after my remaining knight, who jumped out of the way of all his attacks. If he really thought the Vietnamese Communists were that mindless and robotic, maybe he had the right ideas after all. The Communists were regimented, controlled, a bunch of heartless machines who didn't care about the individual life. Everything was secondary to their stupid cause. "Anyway," Sammy said, "what are the Americans doing there?"

"What are you talking about?" This sounded bad.

"If the South Vietnamese don't want the Communists to take over they won't let them."

I realized there was no way he could understand. Being Russian, he had no way of knowing how stupid that statement was. I went after his pawns till his wall collapsed almost entirely, but in the process I left my king undefended and had to bring both my rooks in to protect him. We were both forced to play more defensively, and neither of us could mount a serious attack. The game would take forever, and we didn't have forever. I had to be home in time for homework and supper; he had to be home when his parents arrived from work, or they'd "freak out." We gave up the game at 4:30 and put the black and cream wooden pieces back into their box. Each side went into its own compartment, separated from the other by a thin square of wood.

"Good game," Sammy said. "We both almost won."

"Yeah, good game." We shook hands and parted. I forgave him, or nearly did, and even felt a little sorry for him. He was like the Russian kids — he'd been taught wrong.

* * *

We would go to each other's houses to watch the TV pictures from the moon: glary, washed out images that we wished would be better-angled, better-focused, more like a science-fiction show, but they were still amazing. We'd even watch the splashdowns, despite the fact the whole process seemed to take forever. That just made it all seem more important.

"At least they don't have commercials," Sammy said as we stared at the growing shaky white spot that would eventually become the command module. "This is too important for commercials."

That sent us into an ever-intensifying exchange of our most hated commercials. "Ring around the collar" was always the winner; nobody could ever top it. "Stinks!" he declared. "Fucking *stinks*!"

His sister was named Irina; he called her Irritate to bug her. She was a typical girl: her room was off-limits, but we'd stick our heads in anyway to laugh at the stuffed animals and pictures of the Doors on the wall. "Jim Morrison is *dreamy!*" we'd tell her. Irina had worse acne than I did, and braces with elastic bands you could see.

Sammy's father was a dentist, and his mother a dental assistant; because they worked late we had his house all to ourselves until suppertime, when they'd sometimes invite me to stay for supper. Before we could eat Sammy's mother muttered a prayer under her breath, and the rest of us were supposed to bow our heads. I pretended to, but refused to do a Christian thing for real even if it was only to be polite. I kept waiting for his mother to try to convert me, but she never brought it up. His father was a balding man with round cheeks and a permanent itch behind his right ear. He always asked us the same question after the prayer: "What did you learn in school today?" I think he asked it as a joke, because he always smiled when Sammy said: "Nothing, again." He had a little bit of an accent—a *Russian* accent—and as much as I feared Mrs. Borodin's Christianity I feared his possible Communism more.

I never heard him say anything against the Americans, but once we were talking about the Apollo missions and he said how sad it was that the Russians hadn't gotten to the moon, too. "It would be better if both went."

"Why?" I asked, aching with suspicion.

"So one country couldn't control the whole thing. The Americans will set up bases there and it will belong to them. That's not right."

"It should be the United Nations," Sammy's mother said. But the United Nations was against Israel … always telling it to leave land that it won fair and square in 1967.

"Eh? Nah! Then they'll argue all the time about it." I was

having a terrible time with a piece of steak that chewed and chewed but never got any smaller. We usually didn't eat steak at my house, or at least not myself and my sister; we preferred chicken. "No, the two superpowers should be there. Maybe they'll stop fighting."

And Communism will never be wiped out once and for all, I thought. That's what he really meant. I carefully spat the piece of meat into my paper napkin when nobody was looking, and ate the mashed potatoes instead.

"Anyway, it's too bad about Yuri Gagarin."

My ears perked up. Yuri Gagarin had died in an accident. He was the first man in space, and unfortunately he'd been a Russian. I felt no sorrow over his death. Mr. Borodin shook his head sadly and made a low, "Huh huh huh" sound.

Mourning a Russian hero. I ate quickly and went home soon after supper, telling them I had a lot of homework to do. I wondered if I should ever go over there again—but if I didn't, that would cause too many questions. I'd just have to be strong, and watch for brainwashing.

* * *

That spring came a big announcement: Canada and Russia would play in a hockey series, our best against their national team. It was generally agreed that it would be no contest. Imagine: Bobby Hull, Gordie Howe, Bobby Orr, all on the same team … Jean Beliveau had retired, and there was a question over whether players who joined the new league, the World Hockey Association, would be allowed to play. But Canada had the best players in the world; the Russians wouldn't have a chance.

"We'll cream them," Sammy said. We were at the Chess Club, and nobody was playing chess. Mr. Sandor was in the corner trying out an endgame using a knight and a rook. "It'll be a fucking massacre."

"I don't know why they're bothering," Jerry Kalter said. "But maybe it's just like an exhibition." Exhibition games didn't mean anything; they were like practices. Maybe it was all part of how we were trying to become more friendly with the Russians. Richard Nixon was making friends more and more with the Chinese. "Co-existence," the newspapers were calling it. For my father, it was just appeasement. "It's Chamberlain all over again," he said. I thought so, too.

Once we beat the Russians they'd realize who was better. We hadn't fought them in a war yet, so they still thought they were just as good as us; this would show them. They'd learn.

"They won't be so easy," Sammy said. "They win the world championships all the time."

"So?" I asked. "Who cares? The World Championships don't mean anything." Canada's national team was made up of players who weren't good enough to get into the NHL.

"I know. I'm just saying it means they're not that bad. We'll beat them, but they should still do okay."

"You're nuts," I said. "This is the NHL! And it's *our* game!"

"I didn't say they'd win," Sammy said. "Jeez. I'm just saying they'll stink, but they won't stink that much."

"You're crazy," Jerry said.

Jerry and I made lists of the players we thought should be on the team, producing a dream roster you'd never see even on an All-Star team. Hull, Howe, Mahovlich, Cournoyer, Orr ... we'd show the Russians how to play hockey; things would be settled, in one area, at least, we'd make it very, very clear.

And if Sammy couldn't understand that, it was just too bad.

* * *

We had to write provincial exams in June, and now we had to study for them, so I couldn't spend too much time at the Chess Club any more. The matrics were frighteningly official things; they were held in the gym, and featured printed question books and sometimes computer answer sheets. Most of your mark for a course was based on that one test. When Sammy, Jerry, and I got together it was to quiz each other. I really needed help with my physics; I could never get the equations. I understood basic ideas like gravity and light, mostly because of my interest in space, but the math sometimes stumped me. I was good in English and helped them with that. Mainly, though, I spent hours on my own reviewing my History and Geography and French texts. I'd show the government, too; they were French, and I was English, and there were always times when you felt you needed to show the others how good you were.

Sammy and I met a few minutes before the History matric to throw questions at each other. "What year was the Battle of the Plains of Abraham?" "What year did Royal Government start in New France?" We entered the gym and took our seats. I imagined we'd just gone to the moon together—someplace exciting and dangerous, where we could triumph or die. This was where we'd show what we could do. It was better and worse than chess. Sammy gave me the thumbs up sign, and I returned it.

I ought to have been happy to see us both do well, but I couldn't forget who and what he was. Somehow, it was important that I beat him, just as it was important that we beat the Russians in hockey and everything else, to defeat our enemies because it was right and it was necessary. I wanted to forget who his parents were and what they were like. Only a tiny voice nagged at me, and I wished I could pull that out of me like a splinter. But when I looked over at him I couldn't help wondering: When the hockey games started in September, who would he root for?

"Begin!" Mrs. Young called from the front of the gym.

* * *

That summer, we played lots of chess together, and my determination to win sometimes made me careless. I went for mates, not just wins on points, and I would even throw away pieces thinking I could set up an inescapable trap. He'd always find counter-moves that ended up crushing me, and I tried but failed to be a good loser. In my darker moments I imagined he played with me only because he knew he could win.

When the matric results came back, we learned that we'd both done pretty well; our grades in English Literature were almost identical, though I was in Enriched rather than regular English so I figured that counted for something. I did moderately better in History, while he did better in Math. We both got just low 70s in French.

"French is so fucking boring," he said as we discussed our grades. "Hate it."

"Yeah. It's a waste of time."

Then he went off to work as a camp counsellor and I

played with other guys from the club or I stayed in my room and read science-fiction novels. I borrowed *Dune* from him just before he left and spent days going through it, amazed at how Herbert was able to create a whole world, a complete alien environment and culture. Arrakis became alien and familiar all at once, and I knew I'd never again be able to take seriously shows like *Star Trek*, where all the natives of a planet were alike. I played a few games with Jerry, and he beat me almost every time. But what we concentrated on was the hockey series, not our kings and bishops. He agreed with me: We'd kill the Russians.

When Sammy came back, we got together at my house. "*Dune* was great!" I said as I handed it back to him, its spine now curved and creased beyond repair.

"Yeah. After this everybody else stinks." he said.

"I read lots of Heinlein, too. Great stuff."

"Yeah. *Starship Troopers!*" As we played, he told me about where he'd worked, a camp run by a couple of Russians his father knew. I fought down the crazy images I had, of marching and indoctrination.

School was starting up soon, and we discussed the courses we'd selected. We were in the same homeroom, but not much else together; he was in regular biology and Intro to Business, while I chose some of the higher-level courses like BSCS Biology and Chem Study. We had the same French class, with Mr. Magid, but different interest courses. I couldn't figure out why he'd take Computer Science instead of Directed Reading, which meant doing nothing for a period.

But all we could think about that September was hockey. As we'd feared, the WHA leached players like Bobby

Hull and Gordie Howe from the line-up. Even J.C. Tremblay, my favourite Canadiens defenseman for years, was now in the WHA, abandoning the real league just so he could earn more money.

"We're going to wish we had them," he said.

"You're nuts." It wouldn't matter—we were too good.

"I'm telling you."

"And their goalie stinks." That's what the papers had reported. "We're going to win every game 15-0."

He just shrugged.

What did he know? I couldn't wait for that series to start. We'd show the Russians how to play hockey, we'd show them what the world was all about.

* * *

I was at the Forum that Saturday before school started, for the first game of the series. It was also the first hockey game I'd been to with Dad in years. Canada scored two goals early, and it seemed like it would be so easy. Then Russia started passing the puck around as if they were playing keep-away with us, and as they scored again and again I watched in absolute shock. It couldn't be happening—but there they were burying pucks behind Ken Dryden, and I felt as if I'd been punched in the stomach. The Russians won 7-3.

"Unbelievable," my father said as we left the Forum, pushing our way through the nearly silent crowd. He shook his head over and over, his forehead covered with sweat and not only because the Forum had been a steambath in the early September heat. "Son of a gun. Unbelievable."

I didn't want to see Sammy too soon after that, because I knew he'd say: "I told you so," and I couldn't be sure that he wouldn't be cheering, secretly, somewhere inside. But as it turned out, he was truly angry. I talked to him after French class on the first day, when we finally had a break after finding our way from one class to another, meeting our new teachers and getting our textbooks. The French classroom smelled as if the windows had never been open.

"Do you believe those jerks?" He stabbed the cover of the French book with his forefinger. "Fat. They're all fat. The Russians are in shape, and our guys spend the summer sitting around doing nothing."

"I know. It's not fair. It's not the season yet anyway. They're not supposed to be in shape."

"Why not? The Russians train all year round."

"'Cause they have no choice." They were robots, machines, made to work all the time. That's what Communism was all about. "They'd be sent to Siberia if they didn't."

He smiled at that, and for a moment I wasn't sure if it was because he agreed with me, or if he thought I was being stupid.

The series got worse. We beat them in Toronto, but not in Winnipeg or Vancouver. We almost beat them in the first game in Russia, but then blew the lead. Now we watched the games in school, on those small TVs in cream-coloured cabinets that stood high up on chrome wheeled stands, or the small portable TV that Mr. Magid, our French teacher, brought in. School stopped cold during those games; they meant everything.

* * *

A few days after the game in Vancouver, my father received a strange letter from his mother in Chicago. We were at the supper table when he opened it; he now went out often, trying to get more business, and this was his first chance to see it. Inside the fat white envelope was another, smaller blue one. I recognized it as an airmail envelope: tissue-thin and crinkly. The stamp on it said "Magyar Posta": I knew what that meant. Dad read Bubby Teitel's letter before opening it.

My sister was busy talking about one of her teachers. "She's such an idiot. She can't control a class. She —"

"Shh!" I'd never heard my father shush her like that. She looked deeply insulted, His eyes widened as he read. "*Tzuh!*"

"What is it, Hank?"

"Just a second." He lifted the airmail envelope, which had already been slit open. Inside was one sheet of powder-blue airmail paper, folded in perfect quarters, on which someone had typed those long Hungarian words, then penned accents over the vowels. "*Oy,* Jeez," he breathed. He leaned his elbow on the table and buried his mouth in the base of his palm. "My God. Jesus Murphy."

"Hank!"

"You're not going to believe it." He turned the paper over and over.

For a moment nobody said anything. I got truly scared; I'd never seen him like this, stunned and distant, as if he'd receded far from us and was threatening to fall away altogether.

"My Auntie Ellen. She had a cousin."

"A cousin?" My mother gave a puzzled look. "What cousin?"

"From her father's first wife. He disappeared during the war, and they figured, that's it. My parents just got this letter ..." He waved it at my mother. "It's from him."

"What?"

"They all figured he was dead. Now suddenly out of the blue ..."

"That's crazy." My mother instinctively reached for the blue letter, but then realized she wouldn't understand a word and lowered her hand. "It's a trick."

"No. Maybe." He put the letter down and stared at it as if it would answer his questions. It just lay there waving in the breeze from the oscillating fan in the corner. "Him she didn't talk about, not at all."

Another relative? Another *Hungarian* relative? No one could have survived the war, not like this. Suddenly a letter crossed the Iron Curtain, written in "our" language and the language of our enemies, and we didn't know whether to believe it, trust it.

"What does your mother think?"

"She says he knows things only Gabor would know. But how can you tell for sure?"

"Why all of a sudden?" my mother asked.

"That hockey series. It's all over the news there. He was told he might have relatives in Canada so he contacted some people he knew and traced my parents."

"What does he say?" Sheila asked. She picked up the letter, even though she knew less Hungarian than my mother, who knew only three words.

"Nothing, just asking questions if we're related to so-and-so and such-and-such."

"Write to your parents," my mother said. "Get some answers. Or phone them."

"Yeah, I'll do that." He phoned them on the weekends, usually Sunday depending on his work schedule. But he gobbled down his supper and went into the hall where the telephone table was. I didn't know whether to go out there with him, or stay in the kitchen. My mother leaned against the doorway, watching him dial, and I didn't feel I should push by her, so I listened from my place at the table. The whole house felt different, alien, as he spoke, or rather shouted, those Hungarian words into the phone. Long distance calls were always a big deal because they were so expensive, and my father spoke quickly, asking questions and nodding sharply at the answers.

"*Igen, igen. Köszönöm. Szeretlek.* Bye-bye."

My father hung up the phone, and I could see his lips tighten. He began to blink, in a way I'd never seen him do before. For a moment I thought he'd do something horrible, embarrassing and wrong.

"I'll write to Gabor," he told my mother. I couldn't tell what he was feeling, whether anger or pain. It struck me that I'd seen so little of him lately I might not be able to tell the difference any more. "I'm going to see. I don't want to tell Aunt Ellen anything till I'm sure."

* * *

We watched Game 8 in the French room, crowded around Mr. Magid's portable TV. When Paul Henderson scored we exploded; Sammy and I and the other kids shouted: "Yeah!"

and our arms shot up. We couldn't cheer loudly enough, we couldn't believe the comeback had actually happened even though I, for one, could never really believe we'd actually *lose*. The Russians were evil, and barely human in the way they played, and they'd bought off or intimidated the refs. The odds were all against us. Yet there it was: Henderson shooting the puck past Tretiak again and again on replay.

Sammy, of course, cheered every bit as loudly as I did, and the stupid voice inside that wondered if it was all an act shamed me. I hated the voice, and vowed I would do whatever I had to to make it up to him, even if he didn't know anything about it. Even if it meant not minding when he beat me at chess.

The following day an airmail letter came directly from Hungary. My father managed to ignore it throughout supper, then went out to the porch to read it. I think it was the first time ever that I didn't feel like going out to sit with him, that I had no place there. My chest ached as I watched him through the living room window, looking so far away as the cigar smoke rose and he read the letter for what seemed the tenth time. When he came back in he headed straight for the table in the hall. I watched him swallow and lick his lips.

"I better go over there," he said, to no one in particular. He picked up the phone, and dialled with a stiff index finger, measuring each spin of the dial as if he'd never dialled the number before.

"Ellen *néni*, hello. Hank *vagyok. Igen, igen. Nekünk van megbeszélni valò dolgunk. Atjöhetek?*"

He put the phone down, and without looking at us went toward the front door, reaching into the closet to get his jacket. As the door shut behind him, I knew the borders and lines were crumbling, and I wasn't sure what to do, or think, or feel. I would never get used to hearing him become this other person, this man who could speak the language of a foreign land, the land of our enemies and our family, a land I'd never seen.

Telescope

WHEN I WAS sixteen, my Dad bought a telescope from a friend of his. I could tell as soon as I saw it that it wasn't a very sophisticated model; it didn't have the right-angle mirror for the eyepieces or the equatorial mount that I saw on telescopes advertised in the science-fiction magazines. It came with only one fixed eyepiece, and you adjusted the magnification by extending and contracting the whole eyepiece assembly. My father didn't have anything like a shed that could be used as an observatory, so he would carry it out on clear nights and set it up on the lawn. It stood not very high on its splayed chrome legs, and he would twist himself under it to look up at stars, planets, and whatever nebulae were visible in the washed-out sky of a city.

He would let me look through it once he'd done gazing at the Andromeda Galaxy, or the rings of Saturn, but often whatever he wanted to show me would have moved out of the field of vision by the time I scrunched down under the scope to see it. Even when I did see something, the tiny pin-prick of light would shiver madly in the wind, and I'd have to wait for it to settle before I could tell what it was. The first time I saw Saturn I wasn't sure what I was seeing; it looked like a tiny yellow oval with two black crescents in it. My father explained that the rings were at maximum in-clination, meaning they were angled down so you could see as much of their surface as possible. Those crescents, he told me, were the gaps between the innermost ring and the plan-et. When I understood what I was seeing I actually let out a gasped "Oh!"

That night I dreamed I was standing out in a field at night, and could see Saturn hanging over me looking exactly as I'd seen it through the telescope, only much bigger. The sky was filled with objects I shouldn't have been able to see with the naked eye: fuzzy nebulae that I knew were globular clusters, spiral galaxies, a red ball I could tell was Mars, even the Milky Way as a pale white ribbon.

I was still young enough to tell my parents about my better dreams, and when my Dad heard about that one he said: "Wish it were that easy, eh? You wouldn't need a tele-scope at all."

I knew that "telescope" meant "distant viewer," that it let you see distances. To be able to see the universe without a telescope, I thought ... imagine what distances we'd see.

I'd learned enough astronomy from Dad's magazines and my own that I didn't need much tutoring from him. Thanks to books and a small sky atlas, I knew my way around the constellations better than my neighbourhood, which we'd moved into four years earlier but I still thought of as our "new" one. Of course, seeing pictures in books was nothing like seeing the real things through the telescope, even if the objects were always disappointingly small, and sometimes just tiny smears.

The astronomy books kept referring to "the heavens," which I found strange. Why would scientists call the sky "the heavens," a term out of religion? When I was small and read the term in *The Boy's First Book of Stars*, I wondered if someone thought you could aim your telescope up there and see God sitting on a cloud. Back then, I pictured two completely different skies—one with God and angels in it, the way we were taught at school, and one with nothing but stars and planets, outer space, the way we were *also* taught at school. The two skies never came together. And the telescope made me think of that again, made me wonder once more about the two skies and which one I was supposed to see.

* * *

Astronomy was one of the few hobbies my Dad had left then. His bookkeeping clients were constantly coming through the side door to bring or pick up ledgers. My mother made refreshments for them, so the basement was always filled with the smell of coffee and of the carrot cake or sugar cookies she served with it. The office was a little room near the side door; the rest of the basement was dominated by an old chesterfield and TV we put down there so we'd have a cool place to go on summer nights. It would have been great to have the whole basement for playing in when I was younger, but I'd had to keep my cars and soldiers out of the way of the clients. I considered that terribly unfair, because when my father bought the house he tried to convince us we'd love it by touting its great basement. But we almost never got to use it, and even when my mother had her B'nai Brith meetings down there on Sunday afternoons — the women sitting on padded steel folding chairs around a bridge table — she had to be careful not to interfere with the business going on beyond the closed office door. And the old TV always had to be kept on low. Even when we watched the newer one upstairs in the living room, we had to keep the volume down. Before my sister went off to work at camp, we spent lots of time watching repeats in the stifling hot living room, when we weren't in our separate rooms listening to music or reading. Even with the windows open and the kitchen screen door providing a cross-breeze, the house would be a steambath.

While Dad worked in the basement, I spent the days lying in my back yard reading, or listening to music or Expos games. Sometimes I would set up our folding chaise under the oak tree in the corner of our property, and between stories in a magazine or chapters in a novel, I would look up at the sky through tiny chinks in the leaves. If I squinted, the bright spots became a dense field of stars against a solid black background, and I could almost imagine that I was seeing constellations the way they were meant to be seen: beyond the veil of an atmosphere and Montreal's light pollution.

Some days I played baseball at St. Louis Park with the guys from Sir Winston Churchill High — whoever was around, that is. Most of the kids I went to school with were working in their fathers' businesses or as camp counsellors, so I was pretty much alone that summer. Even my mother had little time for me; she was spending so much of her days helping my father out she seldom had time to speak to me, except at lunch.

"You don't want to do anything this summer?" she asked me not long after school ended. She was at the stove heating up my Beefaroni; she knew I was perfectly capable of preparing my own lunch, but insisted on doing it if I wasn't fast enough to reach the stove before her.

"No." I knew it was time for me to get a summer job, but I was caught up in a kind of inertia; I didn't want to make the effort, even to decide what to do. I was hoping, I expected something was about to happen—I had no idea what. "I'm fine."

She had no answer, and I wasn't sure if she was worried about me or frustrated with me. Was I just being lazy? I couldn't be sure myself. Maybe I was going crazy and didn't know it. That day, my father was out picking up ledgers. He seldom joined us for lunch anyway, usually eating out or at his desk downstairs. He was gaining weight, too, and over the weeks I'd watched with awe as his paunch grew over his belt.

"What's Paul doing?"

"I don't know. Working somewhere." Paul Schneider disappeared not long after school ended; as far as I knew, he was working in a town up north—St. Jerome or something like that. Sammy had a job in his aunt's store, and I also hung out with Jerry Kalter a fair bit. Jerry was one of the few guys from Sir Winnie still around, and he frequently joined the baseball games. Baseball was all the rage, since the Expos had just been formed a couple of years earlier and seemed to be getting better every year. Jerry had been in my Intro to Physical Sciences class, so I could sometimes talk to him not just about baseball but also about what my father and I had seen through the 'scope.

Ma made a bowl of Cream of Wheat for herself, pouring cold milk into the steaming mound in her bowl. She'd had that for lunch almost without fail for as long as I could remember. She had so many habits and rules, traditions that were everything to her, and by now I was used to them —used to seeing them as hers, not anything I wanted any part of.

"All your friends are gone," she said. "I'm surprised you don't miss them."

I shrugged. I did miss them, yet at the same time I felt I needed the solitude, the quiet.

"Okay." Fortunately, she dropped the subject. I was afraid she'd push me into doing something, or even—worst of all —ask me to help out with the bookkeeping, although I couldn't imagine what I'd be able to do, anyway. During the school year I always had things to tell her about; now, I knew I had nothing to say—certainly nothing that wouldn't be utterly boring, or incomprehensible to her. After lunch, she went into the living room to watch *Secret Storm*, her one indulgence before she would have to return to the basement and those ledgers.

* * *

From the time we moved into the new house, my father's business expanded quickly, and his clients—most of them Jewish, Hungarian, plus my uncles and a few French Canadians—began to come in a steady stream, taking up positions on our old chesterfield awaiting their turn like patients at a dentist's. I sometimes came downstairs just far enough to see how many there were. I was impressed by the numbers and at the same time disappointed that the basement was becoming so fully off-limits. Once in a while I had to get a book or other item I'd left downstairs, and would have to retrieve it under the clients' watchful, bored gaze. Except for my uncles, I didn't know whether I was expected to say hello to them or ignore them. The best thing to do was just stay out of the basement altogether.

Most of my father's clients ran factories in the old neighbourhood where my mother grew up, around St. Lawrence Boulevard, or stores on Victoria and Van Horne, and Dad continued to do the books for the printers he worked for before starting his own business. But one of his clients was a rabbi, who brought the *shul's* books to him because my grandparents had been members. It was strange coming home after a baseball game to see Rabbi Lehrman sitting among the other clients on the chesterfield, clutching the huge ledger that you opened with a key, like tins of corned beef. He would always nod to me if I happened to come downstairs while he was there.

"Good afternoon, Lawrence," he said one day.

"Hi."

"Everything is fine?" He nodded whenever he spoke, and I imagined that over time his short beard would scrape the collar of his shirt to shreds.

"Sure." I felt terribly guilty whenever I spoke to him. As a kid, I'd been determined to be a good Jew, a much better one than my parents, but I stopped going to Hebrew School even before I had my Bar Mitzvah, and my enthusiasm for the effort faded. I couldn't bring myself to go to *shul* every Saturday the way I'd planned, especially if my parents didn't go, too. I still prayed, as I lay on my back waiting to fall asleep, although not every night as I used to. Once in a while I said something to Him, just to keep Him aware that I knew He was there. Somewhere.

"What are you doing this summer? Camp?"

"No." I'd gone to Camp B'nai Brith every summer, but decided against it this year. I was too old to be a camper, and I didn't want to work as a counsellor. Summer was for fun, for rest, not work. I could start earning money next year.

"You're not bored?" The other clients listened to the conversation while pretending not to.

"No." Actually, I was sometimes, but it was a small price to pay for my freedom.

Rabbi Lehrman smiled and nodded again. "As long as you're happy."

I wasn't that, but I didn't think I could tell him what I was feeling, even if I'd wanted to.

* * *

Since I knew what I was doing, Dad let me take the telescope outside on my own while he was busy with an after-supper client. There was one spot on the lawn where the scope was shadowed by the house from all streetlights, not too close to the house's own lights, and far enough away from the oak tree, which was wide enough to block out a good range of the sky near the horizon. But out of the corner of my eye I could still see a strip of light beaming through the narrow office window. I had to shield my eye as I hunted down an obscure nebula by following one star to another to another, although usually I couldn't be sure I'd really found what I'd been searching for. I needed to be out in the country, away from the city lights, so I could see farther, see more dim and distant objects.

I always spent far longer out there than I planned to, as I searched, adjusting and readjusting the 'scope; before I knew it, two hours had gone by and I'd only managed to see one or two things. And there were moments of silence when I could easily imagine that the blanket of air between me and the stars was gone, and I saw them clearly through light-years of pure vacuum.

I was using the telescope so much more than my father that it pretty much became mine. That had happened to some of my father's other things, like the chess set my father bought because it was so elegant-looking, with ivory-like, intricate kings and queens, and rooks that were elephants carrying detailed towers on their backs. I "inherited" the little jars of paint left over from a paint-by-number set my father had not had time to finish. The telescope became my property, one of my favourite possessions. During the day, I looked for sunspots, using typing paper clipped to a piece of shirt cardboard as my projection screen. At night, I hunted obscure nebulae and clusters. One night I spent two hours looking for Uranus. When I finally found the hazy little blue disk—barely distinguishable from the sky around it—I punched the air in triumph. I stared at the shimmering pinpoint, then averted my eye slightly to see it better, as the astronomy books recommended. This was the first object I'd ever found that was definitely invisible to the naked eye; without a telescope, the Earth and Uranus were too distant even to know of each other's existence. In a sense, Uranus wasn't really part of our sky, and we weren't part of its.

On those days with no baseball game to play or listen to, those nights when clouds covered the sky, I spent hours reading Asimov, Heinlein, Ellison, Clarke. Their characters lived in far-off worlds, protected from the elements by machines that almost never failed them. I used those magazines and books to look at the other side of the planets and stars I saw through my father's telescope—the side that I knew wasn't real, and probably never would be, but the one that kept me going back to the telescope, even as my father came more and more to abandon it. In fact, by now I'd seen more than he ever had. I would have loved to show him Uranus, or the vague dot I firmly believed was the Ring Nebula, but I didn't dare disturb his work.

The day after I found Uranus I told Jerry about it, and he said: "No way you did that."

"Sure I did."

"Seriously? Prove it."

So I invited him to come over on the next clear evening. He was quite a bit taller than I was, and I had to take that into account as I set up the scope over one of our wooden folding chairs in the back yard. I adjusted the legs of the tripod so that while I might have to crane my neck a little, Jerry would be reasonably comfortable. While I set up, he looked at the stars, clearly lost as he tried to figure out the constellations. "Where are we looking, anyway?"

"Taurus. First I want to show you Saturn."

"Can you really see the rings and everything?"

"Yeah." It suddenly became important to impress him,

even to teach him, to show him what I had seen. "You see that blob of stars there? That's Pleiades." He tried to follow my finger. "Oh, yeah, up there. Right."

"Saturn's right near it."

Unfortunately, Saturn was almost directly above us, and that meant we had to get practically right under the 'scope to see it. Finding Saturn was the smaller challenge; the bigger one was manoeuvring the telescope on its jerky mount so that it stayed aimed at the planet. I missed a couple of times and had to start over; meanwhile, I could feel Jerry getting a bit impatient behind me. My neck ached from leaning forward, but I finally got Saturn lined up, and expanded the eyepiece mount to increase the magnification. When I got the planet focused again and it gleamed steadily at the bottom corner of the field, I quickly slid out and said: "Okay, get under there. And take off your glasses."

He plunked down in the chair, and brought one eye as close to the eyepiece as he dared, covering his other eye with his hand. "I see something. It's just a blob. I thought you said you can see rings."

"You can. Okay, do you see two dark crescent lines inside the blob?"

"Yeah."

"That's the separation between the rings and the planet."

"What? Oh, yeah! Man! Shit *la marde*! It's going out of the field of view there. Wow."

I thought that maybe I should have saved that for after Uranus, because I knew any other planet would be a letdown after Saturn, especially one as dim and dull as Uranus. But he still muttered, "Wow" over and over, and I knew he'd experienced what I did when I first saw Saturn. I looked around for Ophiuchus, and the brighter stars I knew would lead me to the target. It took me sweep after sweep, loosening and tightening the mount over and over again, tracking stars then losing my way. To keep Jerry from becoming impatient I pointed out other sights he could try to entertain himself with, like the Northern Cross and Cassiopeia. When I had Uranus at last, I said: "Okay, get in there fast!"

He sat down and looked through the eyepiece once more, but this time shook his head. "I don't see anything."

"Not even a little blue disk?"

"No."

I took his place at the 'scope; the planet was gone. We tried three more times, but each time he couldn't see it. Either he wasn't quick enough, and the planet had floated out of view by the time he got there, or it was too dim to make out unless you knew what to look for. Maybe our eyes were so different in strength so that what was clear to me was blurry to him.

"You sure it was there?" he asked.

"Yeah. Tiny blue disk—"

"I believe you. I wish I'd seen it."

And I wished that I'd been able to show it to him, that I had a better 'scope or mount, or a darker sky. Far from the city lights and trees, the sky would have been black and sparkling with countless stars, dim and distant ones that were utterly invisible where I lived. I'd seen that kind of sky while at camp, though I wasn't outside too often at night there, and usually when a fire wrecked my night vision. I yearned to see the night sky the way it really was, the way it was meant to be seen.

I showed him a couple more things — we split the double star at the bottom of the Northern Cross, and saw a bit of the Hercules globular cluster. Then he rubbed his neck and said: "That was great. Seriously." He looked back up. "Wow." I wondered if he'd dream, too, of a ringed planet hanging over his head.

I'd run out of easy finds, and we were getting cold, so we decided to go in and catch the Expos game. I loosened the bolts that secured the tripod legs and compacted the tripod, then Jerry held the back door open while I steered the telescope inside, through the kitchen and into my room where I stood it up next to my dresser. I could hear my parents downstairs still working; these days, it seemed as if they only stopped for meals.

We went into the living room and turned on the TV. We found the Expos game on the French CBC — and I made sure to keep the volume low.

"That was great, eh?" Jerry said during the first commercial. "Seriously. Saturn's rings."

* * *

I kept thinking about the two skies, and the idea bothered me more and more. That wasn't something I could discuss with Jerry; I had a pretty good sense he wouldn't know what I was talking about. I tried asking my father at supper, the day after Jerry's visit.

"It's just an expression," he said. "Skies, heavens, same thing."

But they weren't. "Yeah? So why do people say God is everywhere and then keep talking about heaven?"

"Good question. I don't know. Anyway, what's the big deal?"

"It's stupid."

Dad leaned back in his chair and twirled his curly hair around his finger. That was another familiar gesture I'd seen a thousand times. "Maybe it is."

That was all he said. Not only did he not have an answer, it seemed that he didn't even think the question was worth asking. It was hopeless. "Never mind."

"It's, what do you call it, symbolic," he said, to convince me he wasn't trying to dismiss the question completely.

"Everything?"

"What do you mean?"

I could see my mother squirming in her seat as she tried to eat her broiled chicken in peace. But I wouldn't let up. "What's symbolic? Heaven? Everything?" How far would this go? I'd learned enough evolution in school to know the Adam and Eve story was something other than history. Of course, that wasn't the way Hebrew School had taught it. Somehow I was supposed to believe both stories at the same time, and I was getting tired of it.

"I don't know," my father said, glancing at Ma. At that moment he looked more tired than I'd ever seen him. In a way, I thought, it was his own fault—surely he didn't have to keep up the bookkeeping even after supper. But he couldn't turn down a client, no matter how aggravating they could be, no matter how slow they were to pay.

I wondered what Rabbi Lehrman would say if I asked him. He probably faced questions like this all the time, the way Pastor Johnson did each Sunday on his radio talk show on CFCF. I'd heard him a few times responding to callers who challenged the whole nature of religion. I stopped listening when Pastor Johnson said on one of his shows that UFOs were manifestations of the Devil to distract people from God.

The next time Rabbi Lehrman came with his books I went downstairs and waited for him to say hello first. That way I knew I wasn't bothering him.

"Can I ask you a question?"

"Sure."

There was only one other client on the chesterfield, an old Hungarian guy who I knew barely spoke any English. I took out a folding chair from the stack leaning against the laundry room door and set it up next to the chesterfield. "When you talk about heaven you don't mean a place up the sky, right?"

"Eh? No, not quite like that."

"It's symbolic, right?"

"Metaphorical, yes. God is spiritual, not physical. He's not in a physical place like that."

"But he's everywhere."

"Yes, but—"

"So what's symbolic and what isn't?"

"It depends. The bitter herbs you eat on Passover are symbolic—"

"I mean in the Bible. Like Adam and Eve. They didn't really exist, right?"

"Of course they did."

That was ridiculous. "You mean you don't believe in evolution? You think there were really two people in a garden?"

"You think we came from monkeys?"

"That's not what evolution says."

"We were created by God. That's what the Bible says. That's what happened. You think the Bible would lie?"

"No." I didn't know what to say, but I knew this wasn't going anywhere — anywhere that I could go. "I just —"

My father came out of his office then, looking vaguely angry or confused. "What's going on?"

"Nothing," Rabbi Lehrman said. "Lawrence and I are having a very interesting discussion. We'll talk again, eh?" he said to me, but I knew that would be a waste of time. I said "Sure" anyway, to be polite.

My mother came downstairs then with coffee. I was afraid someone would tell her what I'd talked about with Rabbi Lehrman, since I knew she wouldn't be very happy if I bugged the clients. She'd been the one who wanted me to go to Hebrew School, to learn about the traditions and prepare for my Bar Mitzvah. I still remembered where all the holidays came from — who had done what to the Jews, why we had candles for this and different foods for that. I didn't want to hurt her feelings, but I still wanted to ask questions I knew she'd hate. I wanted a thousand different things and nothing, to get answers but not have to deal with what might happen if I asked the questions, all at the same time.

* * *

Over the next few weeks, the constellations shifted, and the planets moved. Some objects became easier to view, others climbed high into the sky, requiring greater contortions beneath the eyepiece. I spent more time staring up into that not-quite-black sky than going to the ball games at St. Louis Park or movies at the Lucerne on Decarie. I considered inviting Jerry again, but I wanted nothing more than to be alone in the quiet, barely feeling the chill that came even on the warmest nights. There was a hollow silence on those nights, once the planes stopped flying into and out of Dorval, when I couldn't even hear the Metropolitan Expressway, or maybe unconsciously blocked it out, and it was as if there was nothing between me and the stars.

There were times during the daylight when I couldn't read, or do much of anything but stare out across the lawn of our back yard—toward the picket fence, toward the narrow, cobweb-shrouded basement window, toward the clouds. I kept looking to the "heavens" for my answer, my choice.

One afternoon, just before supper, I sat on our back stairs trying not to think about it any more, but not wanting to do anything else, either. It was the inertia—I couldn't even get up to go into my room and find something to read. I stared at the oak tree across the lawn, absorbed in the quiet; there was only a light wind, there was no sound from the road. I could see the leaves of the oak flicker in the late afternoon sunlight, and the tree's shadowed trunk became hard and black.

Something snapped.

The tree seemed to recede, fall away from me even as I watched. Everything went with it: the lawn, the houses beyond our fence, the power lines and telephone poles and light standards above the roofs. Or rather, they didn't go with the tree, or anything else; that was the point. They went far from me, and far from each other.

For so long, the world around me had always been *mine*, part of me, like scenery in my own drama. I'd felt it all standing around me, moving and being in response to my vision, my wishes, the things I'd been taught.

But now they were all separate, and far away.

The tree was like Uranus: remote and oblivious, there for itself alone, beyond my vision. I stared at it, as if we were both alien worlds to each other.

The back door squeaked open. "Lawrence?"

I couldn't move to answer my mother. I didn't want her there, but I knew I would be sorry to have her leave.

"It's almost supper. Lawrence?"

I couldn't even turn to look at her, not for a moment, anyway. For the first time in years I felt that pang in my chest, but I pushed it down.

"Is everything all right?"

I finally turned my head, and looked up at her. What I saw was her face in silhouette, and beyond her the sky, looking like a hard blue bowl but it was not a bowl, no matter how much I might see it as one. There was sky, and sky was nothing. There was nothing, infinite nothing, behind her.

"What's the matter? Lawrence?"

I knew that I couldn't answer her, for many reasons. I couldn't speak, not right away. But mostly, I could never tell her—or anyone else, for that matter. But especially her, with all her comforts and protections, the rules and rituals and proper things. Would she even understand? Would I want her to? What would I say—that a sky had disappeared?

"It's okay," I said at last. I looked back at the tree for a moment, and it seemed to be the way it always was: my tree on my lawn near my house. I knew better. I stood up and silently followed my mother into the house, swallowing what I'd seen, holding onto it as if it were precious and terrible, keeping it locked away as if it would destroy her if I breathed a word.

Pallet

"**W**ANNA WORK TODAY?"
I stood in the kitchen in my bare feet, my pyjama top twisted tightly under my arms as I held the phone. "Sure," I said, fighting the daze. My mother looked on, her expression that sleepy look that was so similar to her angry one. I rubbed my eyes with the heel of my hand.

"Be here in a half-hour, eh?"

"Yeah." I hung up and blinked away the sand and burn in my eyes.

"So?" my mother asked. "Another job?"

"Yeah." I was too tired to come up with any more conversation. So I pointed nowhere in particular with my thumb, meaning that I had to get going, and rushed back to my room to dress, noticing along the way that the bathroom door was closed.

I dreaded what I might face that day. I'd signed up at the

beginning of the summer with Pratt Agency, which sent guys out on one- or two-day jobs—some of them awful— all over the west end: Ville St. Laurent, Dorval, Lachine. You never got the call till the morning they needed you, and you never knew exactly what you were going to do till you arrived at the factory, or warehouse, or (on very rare occasions) the office.

I put on my jeans and T-shirt, and pulled apart the slats of my venetian blinds to see what kind of day it was. The wind was strong; dull clouds flew overhead.

"Hey, Lar," my Dad said when I came out of my room.

"Hi."

"Another job, eh? Too bad you can't find anything steady."

"Yeah, I know."

He was wearing the blue suit he always wore, even though he worked down in the basement and as far as I could tell didn't need to dress up, although at least he didn't wear a tie. He'd sit all day at his desk, doing the books for clients who brought the ledgers with them or insisted that he come pick them up along with all the invoices. In a way, I preferred what I was doing. I just did what I was told; I didn't have to hunt for clients or try to keep them happy.

And I didn't have to be "steady." Just as I couldn't explain the jobs to my mother, I couldn't explain to Dad why I didn't want to find anything that would take up the whole summer. I couldn't explain my "inertia," my sense that I couldn't get up the energy to find that kind of job or stick to it. Later, maybe, but not now.

I watched him descend the stairs to the basement, carrying his white "Best Jewish Dad" coffee mug far out in front of him in case of spills.

"Can you have some breakfast?" my mother asked. Her expression had softened as she woke up, but there were extra lines she'd developed only in the past year.

"No!" I half-ran into the bathroom.

"You have to have something," my mother said through the door.

Sure enough, when I came out I found her holding a paper bag. Inside was a bagel she'd prepared for me with a thick layer of pimento cheese between the slices. "Thanks, Ma." I grabbed it, then pulled my jean jacket off the doorknob of the closet door. She'd long ago given up trying to get me to hang it up properly. I pulled on my heavy brown construction boots, the kind that everyone I knew was wearing, even to school. During the summer, I saw little of the kids I knew at school, although one of my friends had told me about Pratt's. But Jerry and I never seemed to be sent out on the same jobs. Maybe the manager thought we'd screw around if we worked together.

"You don't know what you'll be doing?" my mother asked.

With a sigh I said: "No." I'd tried to explain it to her so many times, but she always asked anyway.

"Be careful." She hated these jobs, figuring I deserved better. But this was all you could get if you were a teenage guy; easy work in air-conditioned offices was for girls, like my sister, who was doing filing somewhere.

"Bye. See you later."

I rushed down Noel and up Alexis Nihon. I knew that if I didn't get to Pratt's in time they might give the job to one of the strange guys who hung around every morning. I crossed the muddy field that stretched toward the Metropolitan Expressway, well beyond the houses and high-rise apartment buildings. Pratt's was a squat gray cube sandwiched between the Kraft building and a huge brown warehouse. I took the black iron stairs two at a time and tugged open the steel door. As I crossed the squeaking bare-wood floor I glanced at the middle-aged guys sitting on benches on either side. Some of them, bizarre little men with red noses, looked too drunk or maybe hungover to ever be worth sending on a job. It was a good thing my mother had no idea what the place was like. I'd sometimes tell her a little about the jobs afterward, if I thought she wouldn't get too worried about me.

What I mostly couldn't explain to my parents was that I actually liked how grungy Pratt's was. It seemed realer somehow: realer than school, realer than my parents' Ville St. Laurent house. But I wouldn't tell my mother about the place or the drunks, because I knew she'd worry, that she'd be shocked by the guys and the dirtiest jobs; and I wanted Pratt's to be like school: a separate world from hers, as if it were another planet that was alien and mine all at once.

I went up to the counter. The "foreman" (that was what he called himself) sat at a small desk in his usual white shirt with the sleeves rolled up. He nodded and slid the yellow timesheet toward me. "Wait outside," he said in his weirdly high-pitched voice. "The station wagon. There's two other guys with you, eh?"

"Okay." I looked at the company name stamped in blue on the timesheet: Colgate-Palmolive. I had visions of being put on an assembly line pouring toothpaste into tubes. As I walked out the door one of the drunks glared at me. When I stared him down he hobbled up to the counter and started yelling: "I been here since 6:30!"

"Don't give me that shit," the foreman said. "You just sat down."

I went outside, but couldn't see the station wagon; it must have been on a run bringing other guys to their jobs. Pratt's drove its workers out to the clients to make sure they showed up. I couldn't imagine saying yes to a job then just not going; even at school I made sure to be where I was expected to be, I never skipped classes. I sat down on the bottom step. The other guys came around from the side of the building, where they'd been smoking out of the wind: a kid about my age, and a black guy in his thirties, and huge. They spoke French to each other, the kid with a Quebecois accent and the other with a Caribbean one. I couldn't understand a word.

The white station wagon pulled up near the steel fence that separated Pratt's and the warehouse. The driver came out waving a clipboard at us, motioning us to come over. "Come on, come on!" he said, then switched to, "*Venez, venez!*" pronouncing the words even worse than most of the kids in my French class. We piled into the car, the two French guys in the back and me in the front. The driver—I think he was the foreman's brother or something—backed out with a jerk, then gunned the car forward with another jerk. As we climbed the on-ramp to the Metropolitan, I could see my street, though not my house, since it was blocked by a new office tower.

* * *

I wasn't the only one who'd started working that summer. My mother had found a job a month earlier. My father's business had been doing okay, but not okay enough to manage a house, and so over his objections my mother went out and found work in the office of one of his clients. Most of his clients were in the *schmattah* business, as my parents called it: the "rag" trade. Ma worked at a suede and leather place doing general office stuff, like credit and accounts payable, things I didn't understand at all. She would talk about customers and suppliers, which ones were trustworthy and which ones were crooks, and some of them (on both sides) were people she'd known years ago, even grown up with.

"He was never any good," she said about one of the men her company dealt with. "Even as a kid he was always lying, he even stole from Mr. Klein who had the store where we bought chocolate bars."

Women now went on TV saying that they should be allowed to go out and find jobs to make themselves more "fulfilled." Women's libbers complained that staying home wasn't enough for them: They should be able to do whatever men did. But my mother didn't go out to work to be fulfilled. Neither did I. There was nothing "fulfilling" about shovelling chicken parts onto a conveyor belt so they could be coated in batter, fried, and frozen. Or shelving exhaust pipes according to shape and size at a muffler supply warehouse. Or doing inventory: counting cartons of electric parts with mysterious names and functions. Every time I was driven out on one of Pratt's jobs I was both afraid and intrigued by what I might face. The jobs could be dirty or, more often, heavy; I was never very strong, and other workers had one ultimate put-down: "What are you, weak?" I would always end up looking like an idiot if I ever had to carry heavy boxes around. Still, I liked these jobs, because they were so real and because they were only for a day or two, so that if I made a fool of myself it wouldn't matter since I'd never have to see those people again.

And on those days when Pratt's didn't call, and I was home reading or watching game shows, my house seemed weirdly empty. Before she found the job, I could always sense my mother being *there*, even when I was in my room with the door closed, with CKGM playing on my transistor radio, so I couldn't hear her doing the laundry or talking on the kitchen phone to one of her B'nai Brith friends. But now the house was more silent than I could ever remember it, despite the roar outside of the airplanes flying into Dorval.

That was what I felt that whole summer: a silence, an emptiness so complete I sometimes thought the only thing I could hear was my breathing. It was like outer space the way it was described in my science and science-fiction books, the way it was portrayed in *2001: A Space Odyssey*. Sometimes I would go out to our back yard, lie on the folding chrome-and-vinyl chaise that I always forgot to bring in at night, and stare up at the blank blue sky, thinking and not thinking all at the same time.

* * *

We drove down the Trans-Canada, then along one industrial street after another, past low buildings with company names that I sometimes recognized: Spalding, Texmade, Allopharm, Canada Dry; I'd worked for Canada Dry one day, on a delivery truck hauling crates of ginger ale bottles to the back doors of *depanneurs*. The two French guys in the back seat talked nonstop, while the driver kept glancing at his clipboard as he drove with one hand, and twisting his neck so he could see street names. We finally pulled into a parking lot behind a large brick warehouse, and the driver waved us out. "Ask for Mr. Benoit," he said to me. To the others, he said: "*Icitte. Là!*" We all got out, and he spun the car around and took off.

We found an open shipping door and climbed the black iron stairs. The warehouse beyond was dim and our every step echoed. At a narrow desk just inside the door sat a skinny, balding man who looked up at us as if we were invaders.

"*Ouais?*"

"We're looking for Mr. Benoit," I said.

"*Vous êtes les gars d*'Pratt?" he asked, rising, and the young French guy nodded. "*Ben.*" He reached out and we gave him our timesheets. He gave them a quick look, squared them against the desk, and motioned us to follow. "Okay, come on." He led us toward the far end of the warehouse, down a wide corridor between rows of metal shelves holding stacks of cardboard boxes with detergent, toothpaste, and hairspray logos printed on them. Guys of various ages in green company shirts, jeans, and construction boots or Wallabees were walking up and down the rows, some counting the larger boxes, others pushing hand-trucks piled with smaller ones.

We stepped aside to let a forklift by, waiting between two shelves stacked with *ABC* and *Arctic Snow* boxes. We continued to a shipping bay where a lone worker wearing a checked shirt and jeans waited beside the loading dock, smoking a cigarette. Behind him was what looked at first like a huge stack of wood. At the bay stood a boxcar, its open doors revealing a wall of cardboard cartons of various sizes, each containing ten boxes of detergent. The cartons at the bottom were huge and labelled: "Jumbo Size/Format économique." A steel insert covered the five-inch gap between the loading dock and the floor of the boxcar. A fat rope hung in the space between the warehouse and the car, dancing in the wind.

"Jimmy!" Mr. Benoit called out. "These guys are here for today; show them what to do, eh?"

Jimmy threw his cigarette out between the warehouse wall and the boxcar. He was shorter than I was, had long red hair, and was very thin; his cheekbones were as sharp as a skull's. He went over to the stack of wood and pulled off the top set of boards. "All we do is fill up pallets," he told us as he dropped the thing onto the floor. It landed with an ear-splitting *bang*. "That's it." He pronounced his "th"s like "d"s, although his accent was Irish or Scottish more than French-Canadian.

I tried to imagine telling my mother about pallets. Would I be able to describe one? Boards making a flat bed, with others running below ... but maybe she would already know, maybe she'd been inside a warehouse herself some time — but I found that even harder to imagine. For some reason, I couldn't put my mother together with the person who grew up near St. Lawrence, and who now worked there again. She so seldom talked about the worst things of her childhood, although she sometimes dropped hints: of days when there was no heat in the apartment, of living not far from a stable. I began to wonder about the times she'd say: "You don't want to hear about that." I'd always accepted that as a statement of fact.

"*C'est tous?*" the young guy said, pointing to the boxes and the pallet.

"*Oui, il faut met' les boîtes l-bas*," Jimmy said. His French accent was a little better than mine.

We dropped our jackets onto the floor beside the dock and all began pulling boxes off the train car, rocking them back and forth to free them if we had to. Jimmy was careful to select only those of a certain size to put on the pallet. He manoeuvred the boxes into square layers that wasted as little space as possible and ensured no box sat directly on top of another—the technique reminded me of how I built things with Lego bricks when I was a kid, overlapping them so there'd be no risk of a collapse. When we'd constructed a neat chest-high cube, he said: "Now we wait for the fork-lift. *On attend le truck.*"

We stood around just looking at each other till the fork-lift came, lowered the fork then slid it under the pallet, and lifted the cube away. As soon as it was gone Jimmy grabbed another pallet and tossed it onto the floor. We attacked the boxcar again, this time taking out some of the larger boxes. It took two of us to carry each one.

"*Shit la marde*," the young guy commented as he and Jimmy hoisted one of the Jumbos onto the second layer. I wasn't sure I could do this all day, either. But we left most of the Jumbos for later, since they provided steps to get at the higher small boxes.

And that's what we did all morning: We carried boxes off the train and onto the pallet, pushing or heaving them into place and straightening them as best we could. Most weren't all that heavy, and I began to think I might actually enjoy this job. Even as the sweat rolled down my temples, my forehead, into my T-shirt or my eyes, I thought it wasn't too hard, and there was something refreshingly *dumb* about it. I didn't have to think. Compared to the job at Michelin, where I'd had to unload tires—dense Metro tires, huge truck tires—and roll them to giant bins, this was easy.

The French guys chatted during every wait for the fork-lift; I couldn't make out more a couple of words here and there. The young guy kept talking about his girlfriend—his "*blonde*"—while the older guy referred to his "*famille chez moi*." Jimmy, though, was fully focused on his arranging job, sometimes shoving a protruding box into position with his shoulder. He seldom said anything beyond pointing out which boxes he wanted unloaded next. He lit up another cigarette and smoked it between carries—or when a pallet was full—balancing it meticulously on a latch when he had to put it aside. During breaks, Jimmy and I would sit silently on the Jumbos exposed by our work, and stare into the darkness of the warehouse. Despite the shouts that sometimes echoed across the shelves, and the grunts of some machine or other, the warehouse seemed fogged with a dull, sad silence.

It wasn't long before we'd gouged a hole in the wall of boxes big enough to permit two of us to climb into the train car and toss boxes down to the others. That sped up the fill-ing of the pallet, meaning we had longer stretches of wait-ing for the forklift. During one of those long breaks, Jimmy said: "That's it, then. That's how it's done."

"Yeah." I didn't know what else to answer. I looked down at him from my perch atop a stack of 30-ouncers.

"You're from Pratt's, too, eh?"

"Yeah. You, too?" I'd just assumed he was a full-time worker here.

"Sure. For two weeks now. Been here two weeks." He

puffed on his cigarette; the wind coming from the gap around us whipped away any smoke from the cigarette or his mouth. "Ever read Sartre?"

"No." I was stunned. What the hell could he know about Sartre? Jimmy looked no different from the vagrants and the cleaner drunks at Pratt's: badly shaven, greasy hair, too old to be doing this kind of work.

"Jean-Paul Sartre?" I'd never read Sartre, but we'd studied his views a little in Enriched English the past year. "No. But we read a book by Camus last year."

He looked up at me with a brighter expression. "No kidding. What?"

"*The Plague*. It was pretty good."

"Yeah, yeah. That's a good one. I like *The Stranger* better, but there you are." The forklift emerged from behind the shelves, and we waited for it to carry the pallet away. When it was gone, Jimmy went to get another pallet and said: "*The Plague*, eh?"

I climbed back up the box mountain, still puzzled about where he could have heard about such things. For the next load, I threw down what I thought was a box like all the others, and Jimmy said: "Watch it: watch for the print. One pallet for blue, one for black." He told the other guys the same thing in French. I couldn't see why there was a colour difference in the logos but made sure to toss down the right boxes or at least warn Jimmy if one of the others got in the way and had to be piled up off to the side.

The guy my age, who turned out to be Florent, joined me in scrambling over the boxes, spinning them if necessary to check the logo colours; he threw the boxes down to Albert, who was from Martinique.

"Got to be careful with that, eh?" Jimmy said to no one in particular as he circled the pallet of blues, double-checking to ensure no blacks snuck in. "Very important!" He laughed, then retrieved his cigarette from the latch. To me, he said: "Sartre was clear about that: It's all meaningless."

"I'd like to read him someday," I said. I was planning to go to McGill, although I wasn't sure yet what to take.

"Camus." He scratched the back of his head vigorously. "You read *The Myth of Sisyphus*?"

"No."

"Fuckin' brilliant, that is."

* * *

One load later, a loud buzz signalled lunch, and a raucous horn blew outside. We jumped down from the dock to the pavement and lined up at a canteen truck to buy overpriced drinks and sandwiches. I remembered my mother's bagel, but preferred to eat what the others were eating. Jimmy and I sat at an empty bay, while the French guys ate in the train car.

"How long have you been going to Pratt's?" I asked Jimmy.

"Eh? A few months. This job's okay." He rubbed his chin, and I could hear his long, thin fingers scrape against his stubble. "They're all on holiday, you see, so we get some work."

I bit into my cheese sandwich — the cheapest kind they had — which was nothing more than two slices of Kraft Singles between thin white bread. Like me, Jimmy seemed to enjoy the quiet, or at least need it, and we sat side by side looking out across the parking lot to the empty fields beyond. The hot, muggy wind was perfect for my inertia; all I had to do was watch the grass sway, the clouds fly.

"Lovely day, isn't it?" Jimmy asked suddenly, and laughed, then fell silent again. He lit up yet another cigarette and sucked on it till 1, when the buzzer sounded again. He rose slowly and blew a final, hard cloud, watching it scattered into nothing by the wind. Then he led us back to the boxcar.

* * *

We soon pushed far enough into the car to fit two pallets inside; the French guys filled one while Jimmy and I worked on the other. Florent and I climbed and threw, working our way toward opposite ends of the car. I heard Florent and Albert discuss the Expos—they seemed to be arguing over players whose names I recognized—but couldn't make out most of the rest of what they were saying. Meanwhile, Jimmy and I said little more than: "Look out." Or: "Keep them ones for later." At one point, Florent found some little boxes of Colgate toothpaste, and threw one down saying: "*C'pas pesant,*" that it wasn't heavy. So Albert reached up nonchalantly to catch it, and Florent had a good laugh when the true weight of the box nearly sent Albert flying.

"Yeah," Jimmy said, smiling. "Those little ones can fool you, they can."

I found one and threw it down to him, yelling: "Heads up!" Jimmy pretended to be cowering under a falling boulder.

As our toothpaste pallets reached their seven-layer height, a huge drop of water plopped onto one of the topmost boxes, darkening the cardboard. Another landed soon after, and Jimmy grabbed the fat rope, which turned out to be attached to a canopy that accordioned out from the warehouse wall to cover the space between it and the car. As we waited for the forklift, the rain tapped sombrely on the rubber overhead.

"Where do you live?" I asked Jimmy.

"I'm in the Point," he said. Point St. Charles: I only knew it as the poorest part of the city. "Now I'm looking for a place in Lachine." That wasn't much better.

"Sounds ..." But I couldn't think of anything to say that wouldn't sound completely stupid. Those were realer places than St. Laurent, too, like Pratt's; I had vague images of toughness and squalor, a world beyond that of my parents, and my over-soft house.

* * *

At 2:45 the buzzer sounded again for our fifteen-minute break. I had to go to the bathroom, and asked Jimmy for directions, but I might as well not have bothered. The warehouse was a maze, and I quickly found myself lost among the shelves, the piled-up boxes, the caged areas full of filing cabinets, and the idle forklifts. It reminded me of the time I got lost at the Woolworth's in the Wilderton Shopping Centre, back in my old neighbourhood. I must have been about seven. I'd known that shopping centre almost as well as I knew my home; we shopped at the Steinberg's, I got my hair cut at Sam's, my parents bought my birthday presents at Nick's Toy Store. But suddenly Woolworth's had become an alien place—though, in all my panic, I hadn't really wanted the adventure to end, not right away. For a moment, I'd felt as if I'd walked into another dimension. I wanted my mother to find me, but only after a few more minutes.

I had to ask directions three times before I found the bathroom. The buzzer went off again just as I was finished, and I made my way back to the shipping area. I passed green-uniformed full-timers coming out of the small lounge of sorts where they spent their breaks: A thin wood-veneer table with chrome legs stood in the middle of a bare room, surrounded by matching cheap chairs. The warehouse was weakly lighted by small bulbs hanging high overhead that coloured everything a sickly lemon yellow.

After the break it was time to tackle the Jumbos. We had to drag them out from where they were wedged against each other, and rock them along their bottom corners to the pallets. It took two of us to lift each box into position; I wasn't strong or tall enough to do it well, and my back began to hurt. With the smaller boxes, we'd set up a rhythm, but now we began to get into each other's way, bumping into elbows and backs. When the pallets were full we retired to our opposite ends of the car, sometimes looking at each other but mostly staring down at the Jumbos awaiting us. Even Florent and Albert were getting too tired to joke around much.

The wait for the forklift was now more of a rest period, and I took the chance to lean back and look around. We'd cleared enough of the car to read markings on its walls: lines stencilled "OATS" and "BARLEY" ran all the way around the car, and a series of height markers counted by fives ran up the wall opposite the open door. So far, we'd emptied everything from "TEN FEET" up. I glanced at my watch.

"We usually end at four Fridays," Jimmy said.

"Good," I replied. It was just after three, and I wasn't sure if I could manage till five or whenever they usually closed.

The canopy kept the rain out only until it came down hard; then, water began to pour down in a thin sheet near the car. The forklift driver hunched down as he braved the water to get at our pallets, swearing in French as his green shirt got soaked.

The further we worked our way through the Jumbos, the tighter they were jammed together, and we wrestled with them so that we could free them enough just to get grips on them. Jimmy was sweating so hard as he fought with one box that I was afraid he'd have a heart attack.

"Come on, you fucker!"

We tried shoving the boxes around it out of the way so Jimmy could get some kind of grip on it, but they'd been packed in so tight none would move. Florent sat on the Jumbo behind it and tried to wedge the heels of his construction boots into the space between. When that didn't work he brought his heels down hard onto the front of the box he was sitting on; that bared a good two inches of the stuck box. I climbed up and sat beside Florent, and with the two of us pushing out with our heels, and Jimmy yanking with his hands, we succeeded in freeing it. Albert and Jimmy heaved it up onto the top of the pallet.

"Son of a bitch!" Jimmy said. He leaned with one hand against the pallet, panting violently and wiping his forehead with his sleeve. I rubbed at a twinge in the small of my back. "Son of a fuckin' bitch!" He looked up at me and smiled through his ragged breathing. "There you are, eh?"

With a look, I asked him what he meant.

"That's it, then."

When we'd gotten the last Jumbo onto the pallet Florent gave the load a kick for good measure before sitting down. Jimmy lit another cigarette, and after the forklift had taken the load away he took his time getting up to bring another pallet. By now our supply was almost gone anyway. The forklift returned in just a few minutes with a fresh stack: pallets piled up on a pallet. Taking Jimmy's lead, we just sat and watched as the fork lowered, setting the stack gently onto the floor. The truck backed up and turned away, and the stack wavered till it settled, motionless.

At that moment Jimmy burst out laughing, and I glanced into the warehouse to catch whatever it was he'd seen. Finally, I asked: "What?"

I watched his profile as he took a puff. Then he climbed onto a Jumbo, stood up, and struck a pose that reminded me of my Grade 8 English teacher reciting some lines from *Julius Caesar*: arms spread, hands wide open. He made a sweeping gesture and shouted in mock-ecstasy: "What a life! Putting boxes onto pallets!" He laughed.

I laughed, too, but mostly I just stared. The other guys looked at us with smiles on their faces and in their eyes; it was clear they hadn't understood a word of it. I had. I knew exactly what he was talking about. I just couldn't believe that he was the one saying it. The stubble, the ratty shirt … still chuckling, Jimmy said: "Shit," then dropped what was left of his cigarette and toed it out. He went and got us a couple of new pallets, dropping them at our feet.

* * *

A few minutes after our third load of Jumbos was carried away, Mr. Benoit came and said: "Okay, finish'; *c'est tout*." My back hurt badly now, and my hair was stringy with sweat. I collected my jean jacket, feeling the bagel still bulging in the pocket. Mr. Benoit led us back to his desk where the timesheets lay in a neat pile on the blotter. He filled them in so carefully that unlike other bosses he stayed perfectly within the lines. "Six hours fifteen," he said: nothing for lunch or even the afternoon break. We thanked him and headed out the shipping door, into what was now a cold drizzle. Albert and Florent found a bus stop and sat on the kerb to wait, but Jimmy said to me: "C'mon, I know a shortcut to Pratt's."

At first, we went the wrong way, then turned and cut across some soggy fields, through a couple of underpasses, and walked beside the Metropolitan for a while. The cars and trucks above were the only sounds apart from the patter of the rain against my jacket.

By the time we got to Pratt's we were pretty soaked. Because it was Friday, the foreman and Mrs. Pratt were both there, one to take the timesheets and the other to give out the pay for the previous week.

"Hey, Jimmy!" the foreman said. "Still out there, eh?"

"Yeah." He gave me his timesheet. "Would you mind, then?"

"No."

"Here you go, Jimmy," Mrs. Pratt said as she handed him his envelope.

I lined up to hand in our timesheets. The others in the line were guys my age or a little older, and some Jimmy's age. They were all hard-featured, nothing like the kids at Sir

Winston Churchill High. That was right. Even though my back ached it was still an easier day than I'd had before; I hoped I could work at Colgate-Palmolive again. After handing in the timesheets I lined up for my paycheque and looked around for Jimmy, to ask him if he could help me get more work there, but he was gone.

By now, my mother would be on her way home, from wherever it was she spent her days. I hoped she had a clean office to work in, that she didn't mind too much being back in her old neighbourhood after working so hard to get out of it. I would tell her about today's job, but of course I wouldn't talk about Jimmy. She wouldn't understand, anyway.

As soon as I got my envelope I pushed my way through the crowd and out the door. The drizzle had turned into another downpour. Pulling my jean jacket around me, I ran home in the rain.

Distances

DURING MY FINAL year of high school, I got a letter from my old friend, Howard Cohen. He hadn't written me in years; he'd been my best friend in my old neighbourhood, and I still considered him one of my "real" friends, more than the ones I'd made in Ville St. Laurent. After my Bar Mitzvah, when I stopped attending Hebrew school, we exchanged a few letters. It was always great getting those small envelopes with my address in his distinctive scrawl—little changed from elementary school —and the six-cent stamps with the Queen's picture. But then the letters got fewer and fewer; for a couple of years we sent cards on each other's birthdays, and eventually not even that. So it was quite a surprise when I saw the envelope my mother had placed on my bed, with my address typed on the front and Howard's address carefully centred on the back flap.

The letter was on narrow vellum paper and typewritten with keys that needed cleaning; the circles of the "o"s and "b"s were almost completely filled in. It was so typical of Howard, whom I'd thought of as a "*shlump*" (to use Ma's term). The style was the same familiar one, with lots of exclamation marks and sentences beginning with "Well," as if he were writing a composition. And he used the same old first line: "Hello, Lawrence! How are you? I am fine!" He told me he was working part-time in his uncle's warehouse, typing invoices and doing some shipping. He bragged that he was using the typewriter at work for the letter: "I can use it any time I want, except during work hours, of course!" He was getting ready to go to John Abbott CEGEP in the fall where he'd take business courses.

I tried to picture him as a teenager, but I couldn't help seeing the ten-year-old in a coat with a ripped zipper. Working in a warehouse? Becoming a businessman? It didn't seem at all possible.

Most of his letter was made up of news about our old gang. Wayne Fischman was planning to become a dentist, and would be taking science and math at the same CEGEP. Jeff Gold was going to hitchhike around Europe for a year; he planned to be an architect. "He took Technical Drawing at Northmount and was pretty good at it!" Kenny Wasserman had won math prizes and was thinking of becoming an accountant like his father. "Kenny figures he knows half the business anyways; he helps his Dad do income tax returns." His cousin Paul, who had been my best friend when I was very small, was now living in Vancouver and sometimes asked Kenny about me.

"Zvi Rosen is working on a kibbutz in Israel. He got wounded in the Yom Kippur War so they gave him light duties, like cooking. Is that crazy??"

I stared at the words: Zvi had been a kid who loved to take chances, and he'd actually gone to Israel and been in a war ... I was amazed by what had happened to him, and all the others. It was as if there were two of everyone Howard talked about. Would I even recognize Zvi or Wayne or Jeff if I saw them? I had long hair by then, because everyone did, even though I'd once vowed never to look like those "girly" Beatles, and I was trying to grow sideburns. Did the others also have hair to their shoulders? Did Wayne have a beard? Did Kenny carry around a briefcase? And what about Howard himself? Was he still wearing clothes his mother got from relatives or the basement at Ogilvy's? I wanted to reply right away, but couldn't imagine what I'd say. I put the letter down — there was another page-and-a-half to go — and lay back on my bed, staring up at the ceiling and feeling as if I'd heard that someone had died. There was something more, too, that bothered me, but I couldn't put my finger on it.

I read the rest, barely absorbing what Howard said. He asked his usual questions about my family, and in the same order as he'd asked them in his old letters: mother, father, sister. "How is Sheila? Is she still a pain?"

I'd have to reply, but I wasn't sure what to tell him. I'd wait till I had enough to say, and knew how to put it. I planned to make a pun on Kenny's job and tell Howard that I would also be an "accountant," but a different kind: I'd give an "account" of things that had happened to me, a full report. Because if he was willing to write to me after all those years, he deserved that much.

* * *

Unlike Howard and all the rest of my old gang, I had no idea what I wanted to do after high school. Or at least I knew what I felt like doing, but not how to do it. I wanted to explain the world to the world; that's how I put it to myself. I'd always been good at science, and loved to teach what I knew — to my parents when they listened, to my friends when they cared. It annoyed me that there was so much that other people didn't know, so many things all around us that seemed obvious to me and were mysteries to almost everybody else. At high school I took advanced courses like PSSC Physics and Chem Study, and when my grandmother asked me what I was learning in school I wanted desperately to explain it all. She would smile and nod, then seek out my mother in the kitchen before I was done.

"Bubby, there's a lot more to it —"

"It's okay, *ainekel*. I'm too old to understand such things." She preferred to gossip with my mother about our cousins and uncles, about friends. My mother paid slightly more attention to me when I talked about science, but then would say: "I don't have the head for it; as long as *you* understand it." And change the subject.

I wanted everyone to know there were nine planets, there were twelve moons around Jupiter, what a comet really was. The very words "outer space" were magic to me, as they were for my father, who still read science-fiction magazines when he had time. But while he wanted to read about what *might* be out there, I wanted to tell people what *was*. Outer space was just that: space, nothing, *beyond*, vast reaches of vacuum yet full of wonders and truths. I covered the walls of my bedroom with photos I cut out of *Sky and Telescope*, and dreamed of having my own observatory in our back yard one day, with a huge reflector telescope instead of my puny refractor. While my Dad read all of Isaac Asimov's fiction, I preferred his columns in *Fantasy and Science Fiction*, and wanted to be just like him, explaining the twins paradox, how light was both a wave and particle function, how DNA worked. I enjoyed correcting people who didn't know the order of the planets, or who thought a light-year was a measurement of time.

But I didn't want to be a teacher; I couldn't imagine standing in front of a bunch of teenagers like my classmates, dealing with their noise and stupidity. I wanted to write books or articles describing how the universe worked, from mitochondria to white dwarfs. Maybe I'd write a column in a newspaper, replacing the silly astrology page with one on astronomy, on what the stars were really all about.

But I had no idea how to go about it. It wasn't as if I could ask my parents. For one thing, ironically, I saw less of them now that my father worked at home. He spent all day and most of the evening downstairs in the office, emerging only for meals and the TV shows he refused to miss. If I was home while he was struggling with general ledgers and stacks of disorganized invoices, I would heard him swear and sometimes smack the desk. Those ledgers haunted him even during meals; he would sometimes leave the supper table if he thought he'd figured out where the imbalance might be. The longest time he ever took away from his ledger books and invoices was during the hockey playoffs, when we sat in the living room screaming for the Canadiens to score. When he wasn't doing the books he had to make trips and phone calls, to do his pick-ups and deliveries or to hound his clients. They often didn't pay him, or made a fuss about his fee: He called them "the goddamn *schnorers.*"

And my mother now had an office job, then had to cook supper and clean up the house (between visits by our char) when she got home. She'd usually be too tired to do more than complain about Mr. Walderman, or the girls she had to work with. "They have this one girl there, she does filing sometimes, she doesn't pay attention at all, at all. Sometimes I have to go in there and fix her work. No brains. And they don't care." After supper, she'd go downstairs to help Dad.

So they had enough to deal with. I wished I could do something for them: Grab the owners of those dress factories, shake them, warn them, make sure they behaved properly. That was the world, the part of the city, that my parents had both come from and couldn't escape, the old neighbourhood where my mother had grown up and where they'd had their first flat. Colonial, Marianne, Duluth ... that's where Uncle Nat, Aunt Tillie, and cousin Ruth still lived. After Ruth's brother David died, we visited them sometimes; Dad would first make a pick-up or delivery, and the giant ledger books and rubber-banded stacks of invoices tottered on the back seat of the car between Sheila and me. Then we'd drive through the narrow streets with apartment buildings whose front doors were flush with the sidewalks or that had staircases spiralling up the front. When I was sixteen I begged off those visits, but my sister still went, and for a few hours I had the whole house to myself.

Even if I got the chance to talk to them, what would I ask? They didn't know anything about science, writing books, or even what going to CEGEP was all about. My sister had to explain to them what those new colleges were all about, and the difference between the Pre-University and Professional programs you had to choose from.

So what would I do? I figured I'd probably end up going to Vanier College like Sheila. She was taking Social Sciences, and planned to go to McGill to study psychology or sociology and become a social worker. I almost never saw her any more, too, since she spent her time at Vanier or practising with the St. Laurent skating club she'd joined. She was also dating a guy who lived on our block, Harvey Lefkovich, and was usually off with him seeing a movie at the Lucerne or going downtown to one of the clubs on Crescent Street. He was already at McGill, and when he came over to pick Sheila up he seemed so far ahead of me in everything that I had little to say to him, unless it was about the Canadiens.

The deadline for applying to Vanier, March 1, was rushing at me, but I couldn't bring myself to fill out the forms. Not yet, at least. I was supposed to go — it was expected, it was what I expected from myself — but I felt as if I were waiting for something, or that I couldn't move, or that there'd be another path that would somehow open up, although I didn't know what it could possibly be. It was like being on a raft floating past all my landing places, knowing I could never reach them and coming to accept that.

* * *

I couldn't even decide whether or how to tell my parents what I wanted to do. I could just hear my mother: "Write science books? Can you make a living doing that?" She liked everything to be orderly and familiar, and this would be something far outside her boundaries. My Dad would probably stare at me, not sure what to offer but liking the idea—*as* an idea, not as a job. Since they wouldn't know how I could get there, I didn't have to worry about asking them what I should do. I really didn't want them to give me advice. It was my path, and I preferred to go by myself, without their involvement.

But it was hard to find the right time to talk to them. They were so busy I hesitated to bother them. What was the point of wasting their time with things they wouldn't understand anyhow? I so seldom saw my mother actually sit down and talk to Dad, or Sheila, or even her friends any more; the only people she had long conversations with now were Ruth (by phone only) and Bubby. My grandmother visited most Sundays, and during the afternoon she and my mother would talk, almost without a break, in the kitchen over tea and *rugelach* from Cantor's. Nowadays, it seemed, they spent a lot of time talking about Ruth, who was going for tests.

"Are you going with her?" Bubby asked my mother one time.

"She won't let. She can take care of herself."

"Always." As in, Ruth had always been like that, refusing help. I'd never liked Ruth, from the time I was small and she'd been our main babysitter; she'd done things her own way, even when she was taking care of me and Sheila and it wasn't *our* way. I was curious what was happening with her, but Ma and Bubby switched to Yiddish. I kept on pouring lemonade from the big Sealtest carton, slowly, hoping for a switch back to English.

Ever since my grandfather died, Bubby had seemed to get smaller and smaller—and it wasn't just because I was growing up. Her body was shrivelling, and I realized with a shock as I looked at her now that I could pick her up if I wanted to; she was no longer beyond me. Her feet barely touched the linoleum as she sat on one of our chrome-and-vinyl kitchen chairs, and her tiny hands were like those of a child as she cradled her tea glass.

"And your Uncle Sam, he's not well," Bubby said.

"Oh? What's with him?"

"The stomach again …"

"*Oy*. What did the doctor say?"

"Nothing."

Then my mother startled me with a violent dismissive snort. "Doctors. What do they know?"

* * *

Thanks to Sheila, I ended up telling my parents about my plans before I was ready to. We were at the supper table, and Sheila was home that night, since she had to study for a quiz. "Did you apply to Vanier yet?" she asked me out of the blue. I hadn't realized she was paying attention to things like that.

"No."

"How come? Isn't the deadline soon?"

"Yeah."

My father leaned back in his chair. "Eh?" He rested his arm awkwardly on the top of the chair and stared at me over the top of the strange half-glasses he now wore.

"I don't know if I'm going."

My mother looked up and raised her eyebrows. "What do you mean you're not going?"

"I don't know what to do there."

"Just take a whole bunch of stuff—" my sister said, but then she saw how my body shifted, and seemed to recognize that it wasn't a matter of which subject to choose.

"What do you want to do?" Dad asked.

"Write science books. Like Asimov. Or something like that. Articles."

"Write articles? You don't want to be a scientist?"

"I thought that's what you wanted," Ma said, her tone puzzled as if I'd said something incomprehensible, insane. She'd thought that she had me figured out. I stiffened at that, every bone and muscle setting in place. For her, the world was so easy to understand, everything fit so perfectly. But things weren't really like that.

"No," I said, a bit too sharply. Actually, I did want to study science, to pursue astronomy and see more and more through bigger 'scopes. I would also like to do experiments, as I loved to in Chem Study and had so much fun doing as a little kid with Kenny Wasserman's chemistry set, which I'd coveted for a long time. Of course, I knew I couldn't do both. How could I choose between Chemistry and Astronomy, and Physics, and Biology? And even so, it wasn't enough to just make discoveries; I had to share them with everybody. "Like I said, write about it. Maybe for kids, too."

That just came out; I'd really never thought it through before. Write science books for kids.

"For kids?" Ma said. My sister nodded; she seemed to actually like the idea, much to my surprise. But Ma was still having trouble absorbing all this, and asked, as if it weren't clear already, "You mean kids' books?"

I replied with a shrug meaning: Something like that.

"So you'd take journalism," my father said, playing with

his thinning hair as I'd seen him doing so often. Was that it? Take science first, then ... Is that what Asimov and Carl Sagan had done? "It's a tough field, you know."

"I know." But I didn't. It seemed like the right thing to say, though.

"Well, you've got time," he said.

I tried to read my mother's reaction, as she sat silently, assimilating what I'd said. I knew she would have preferred me to take a route that made sense to her: become a doctor, lawyer, dentist like my friends, both old and new, or the sons of her own friends. She'd always wanted an orderly life for herself and all of us. She figured Sheila would end up working for a little while, then get married and have kids, and I figured she'd pictured me in a lab coat, earning lots of money doing mysterious but important work. I didn't want to disappoint her, but I didn't want to fit her images either. Not everything happened according to plans and traditions, to predictions and order. Even in space it didn't work that way. There were laws, yes, but then there were accidents, collisions; there were eruptions; stars suddenly exploded.

"Well," my mother said, "do what you'll enjoy or you won't be happy." *Yes*, I replied silently; but I wasn't sure she really felt that way. I got the sense she said it because it seemed like the appropriate thing to say.

"But what about school?" Dad asked.

"Like I said, I don't know."

There was a deep silence at that, no one knowing what to reply, then Sheila started talking about her own classes and I was very glad for the interruption. Sociology, statistics, weird psychological terms ... it was all as far from what I was interested in as could be. But for her it was vital stuff, and she obviously hated not doing as well as she thought she would.

* * *

If only she could do statistics as well as she could skate. Sheila often appeared as a soloist in her club's Winter and Spring Festivals on Ice, which we had to attend; the little kids were cute, the middle ones funny sometimes, but she was spectacular. She was also on the Vanier skating team, but we never got to see them perform, for some reason. There were technical competitions that only skaters and judges participated in. I was sorry I didn't see more of Sheila then, because I wanted to learn more about what CEGEP was like, for when I would eventually go. Just as with the switch from elementary to high school, it seemed as if Sheila was part of a strange new world; in this one, classes were short and scattered all over the schedule, with big gaps in between. What did you do during the gaps? I thought I could get some idea what to expect by her example, but she was almost never around, thanks to school, skating, and Harvey.

Harvey had a light-brown afro, gold-rimmed glasses, and sideburns, and he drove a Duster he'd gotten from his parents, much to my amazement. I couldn't imagine getting such a gift, even if my parents could afford it. He'd come to pick up Sheila at precisely 6:30, always on Fridays and Saturdays and sometimes during the week. He'd take her to dinner at our favourite pizza place, Sapri, or the Brown Derby in the Van Horne Shopping Centre where he knew the owner. Before leaving, they would sit on our plastic-covered chesterfield, Harvey running his hand back and forth across Sheila's shoulder blades, waiting till my Dad finished trying to make conversation.

"What are you seeing tonight?" Dad would lean against the doorway; he never sat down with them.

"*Serpico.*"

"Isn't that kind of violent?" My sister rolled her eyes at his worried-Dad routine. At least she no longer rolled her eyes at me.

Harvey shrugged. "It's supposed to be good."

"What time will you be back?"

Harvey looked at Sheila questioningly, as if he hadn't planned out the whole night already. "I don't know. 11:30 or 12."

"I don't know, Daddy," Sheila said. "Not too late."

Dad straightened up, letting them know they could go. "Okay, have a good time."

During this whole procedure, my mother remained in the kitchen, preferring not to do anything that might embarrass or aggravate Sheila. It seemed to me she wanted to see this ritual followed through to the end. My parents weren't used to having a daughter who dated; she'd been alone through most of high school, except for her skating friends toward the end. They seemed to be doing what they'd seen parents do on TV: parenting according to *The Brady Bunch*.

Did they know that the Duster pulled up outside our house a half-hour before Sheila came through our door? I'd seen them in there one time when I was out with my telescope; they kissed without pause, practically blurred into one person.

I didn't have a girlfriend yet; the whole idea seemed beyond me just then. There were girls I had crushes on, but they all had boyfriends already, and anyhow I found most of the girls in my class moronic and snobbish. What would we have to talk about? I had too much to figure out now, anyway.

The deadline for applying to the CEGEPs came and went, and I was immensely relieved. Time had solved part of my problem. Now what? The only other choice seemed to be working for a year, but I'd spent enough time in warehouses, and seen enough of what my parents had to put up with, to relish that idea.

* * *

Dear Howard:

Thank you so much for your letter! It was great hearing from you. And thanks for all the news about the gang. I can't believe what's happened to everybody.

How are you? Are you still working in for your uncle? Is it an okay job?

I'm just about to finish at Sir Winnie; the matrics are coming up soon. I'm studying mainly for the science exams. I don't care that much about French or Geography. I like History, though. This year we studied Asian history, especially Japan!

I knew Howard would like the exclamation marks. I then proceeded to tell him about the kids at my school: the bullies, the potheads who hung out in the basement lounge, the slutty girls and the bright ones who took the same advanced courses I did, the guys I was friends with.

Then I told him about my plans, or what there was of

them. I talked about writing science books, maybe training to be a journalist somewhere if that's what it took. There were still a few months left in the year; maybe I could write something for the school paper. I told him about Harvey and my sister, knowing he'd find that hard to believe.

> She's a lot better now; she's more grown up and doesn't try to boss me around any more, although that could be because I'm bigger than she is now. Ha! Sorry for the bad handwriting; I don't have a typewriter like you do. Not yet, anyway.

And then I went through the list of our old friends, and asked for more details about each one. How did Zvi get wounded? Where? What were guys going to study at CEGEP? Where was Jeff going in Europe? Of all the plans, that struck me as the most alien and frightening and exciting: just going around countries where you don't know the language — or not very well, at least — and sleeping wherever you can find somewhere? I could just imagine my parents' reaction if I told them I was going to do *that*!

I said my parents were fine and they sent their regards. In truth, they didn't know anything about my letter, but it seemed like the polite thing to say. I then told him about various other relatives: uncles, Ruth, how tiny Bubby was now. The letter was becoming massive, and that was just fine. I wanted to send a substantial message; it wasn't all that far between Ville St. Laurent and Côte-des-Neiges, but it seemed vital that I fill up the letter with news, and make sure he sent back a reply that was just as full, just as solid.

Anyway, Howard, it was great getting your letter, as I said, and I hope you have the time to write again soon. Let me know how your mother is, and how your job is going. Also let me know what John Abbott says; I'm sure you'll get accepted.

As I sealed the letter, I thought I should have reminded him of some of our adventures, some of our old teachers at Bedford, and even some of the other kids we barely knew but who were in our classes or we had some dealings with. Even the bullies, the fat girls we made fun of, the foreign kids we looked upon as exotic creatures.

Next time, I thought, and went downstairs to ask Dad for a stamp.

* * *

It took me a couple of weeks to realize why I didn't know what to do at school. I didn't want to *do*; I wanted to *go*.

That's what had nagged me so much about Howard's letter: that news about Jeff, all those names from the past and from far away. In the back of my mind I'd long yearned to go away—not for good, of course, not even for long— just long and just far enough. I needed to step away from my parents' rules and all the little ways we did things, all those patterns my mother had set up for us. Hers was a world of certainties and rituals, the clean and orderly world of Côte-des-Neiges and Ville St. Laurent, and I needed to cross the borders for a while.

I wouldn't be stupid or careless about it. I had no intention of hitchhiking across Europe like Jeff, but I saw no reason I couldn't take buses or trains across Canada. Maybe I could go as far as Vancouver and visit Paul Wasserman, renew an acquaintance that broke off in Grade 2.

But if I had trouble telling my parents about CEGEP, how could I explain this? I could hear them now: "Are you crazy?" And if they forbade me, would I listen?

No.

I'd get Paul's address from Howard, write Paul to ask if he'd like a visitor from far away and the distant past. Or maybe I'd surprise him, show up on his doorstep. I had no idea, but I'd figure it out.

Meanwhile, all I could focus on were the matrics. I formed neat piles of my textbooks and notes, arranged in order of my own priorities: PSSC Physics, Functions, Biology, and History, followed by English, French, and Introduction to Data Processing—which I'd taken because of its name—at the rear. The closer we got to the exams, the fewer students showed up for class; I wasn't going to surrender one minute of class time, because I didn't want to take any chances. Not when I wasn't sure what I would end up doing or where I'd do it.

And good marks would help me convince my parents, especially my mother, that I knew what I was doing, no matter how "crazy" my plans seemed.

I finally wrote to Paul a little before my first exam, and he told me he'd be "thrilled" to see me again; he'd always wondered what happened to me, and in his letter he talked about those days of playing cars under his stairs, all the careful routes we'd designed, and the rules of the road we'd established.

* * *

One evening, I came out of my room to find my mother sitting at the kitchen table. I was surprised to find her there; she'd normally be down in the basement at that hour. She'd taken out the family pictures, which she kept in brown paper envelopes on a shelf in her closet, and spread them all over the table. She didn't look up as I came in. I'd never seen her lips pressed so tightly together as she slid the photos around, picking up one here, one there.

"Ma?"

"Eh?"

I sat down across from her, and she pushed a larger-than-normal, white-bordered picture toward me. I picked it up and saw two young girls, about eleven or twelve years old; one of them was clearly my mother.

"That's me with your cousin Ruth." She took the picture back. "We were like sisters. Later she'd always be there. She wouldn't let the French kids bother us, oh, no. 'You know who our uncle is?' she'd say to them. That scared them, let me tell you."

I remembered her stories about the French gangs in the old neighbourhood. She hadn't talked about that for a long time. I didn't recognize the edge in her voice.

"The *chalaria*s knew not to mess with her. She was tough. She didn't have an easy life. Never."

"What's going on?"

"Cancer. Like her brother." She finally looked up at me. "Just like David." I'd never seen her so angry. "No *mazel*. It's not right."

I thought briefly of explaining that it had nothing to do with right and wrong; the world didn't work that way, no matter what we were told, no matter what we were taught —by parents, rabbis, teachers.

She kept pulling pictures out of the brown envelope, selecting out the ones showing herself and Ruth together: standing side by side in long coats in a park, sitting at the same round table at a wedding or Bar Mitzvah. I piled them up for her as she showed them to me, one by one, most of them familiar; I remembered the times she'd take them out and start putting them in order, to organize them for an album, but would soon give up. She handed over one I was sure I'd never seen before: They were inside what looked like a factory, seated at a table covered with small metal bits. They wore kerchiefs. Neither smiled, and their eyes were half-closed.

"Where was this?"

"We had to sort electrical tubes ..."

"Yeah? You never told me about that." In a factory? Her? Incredible—but how could I not have known, or at least figured it out? I'd been to that old neighbourhood so often.

"Eh?" Then, abruptly, "What's to tell?" As if: What's the point, now? But I needed to know this, to find out where she'd been, what lay beneath it all.

Now she fingered another picture, rubbing it with her thumbs. "She was there with me the whole time." She showed it to me: They stood together, and on the border was printed July 1956, and I saw my mother's left hand resting on her belly in that unmistakeable pose. "That was you. She came to the hospital, stayed with me while your father worked for that son of a gun, who wouldn't let him leave the office. Fought with those doctors who were like butchers, who wanted to cut me open."

"It was like that?" She'd never said. She'd kept her silence. I blinked, absorbing this.

"Oh, yeah. Terrible. Without her, who knows what would

have happened?" She shook her head. "And now this. Why? Eh? Tell me why."

There was nothing to tell.

"She had such a hard time, her whole life, and now this. The *chalaria*s don't suffer, but first she loses her brother, and now this." Then, after a pause: "I don't understand."

It was the most frightening thing I'd ever heard her say. I sat open-mouthed across from her, afraid of what I'd see.

She made a vague effort to gather the pictures back together. I was unprepared for what followed. "*Ach*!" I jumped; my heart lurched, and wouldn't slow. I knew then I would never forget that sound, bursting from deep inside her, and the black look on her face as she stared at the table.

* * *

There was nothing I could say to her then, or later, and when I think back on that day I imagine all that I might have said or done if we'd been different people, or if I'd been less shocked. There were things I wanted to tell her, but I couldn't have gotten the words out, no matter what. I've always told myself she understood, and I hope that's true.

I didn't change my plans. As it turned out Ruth was not in any immediate danger, although she had a long fight ahead of her, and there was absolutely nothing I could do, anyway. My mother went with her to the hospital for the tests and treatments, and didn't talk about any of it; instead, she headed right back to the books when she came home, as if nothing were happening. In doing so, she seemed to be the person I'd always known, but of course that was impossible.

After my last exam, I bought my Voyageur bus ticket and I told my parents what I would do that summer and fall. The money I'd saved up for CEGEP went to that ticket and spending money, plus my Dad gave me fifty dollars when it was clear my mind was made up. My mother greeted my news and preparations with looks I couldn't interpret. I thought—or maybe I only hoped—that she understood, that she believed she should have seen it coming. I was sure my sister would think I was nuts, but she didn't seem to care one way or another; school and Harvey took up all her time and focus.

Right up to the day I left, even as I agreed to let my father drive me to the bus station, my mother accepted my going away, never arguing with me, never trying to stop me. I wished she had, to erase what I'd seen and heard.

While I watched my father manoeuvre the car out of our garage, I knew that everywhere I went, every day I was away from home, my mother would be there, as a guide and a challenge. For now, I'd find my own path, make my own space, then come back to see where she was, how far, and how near.

Acknowledgements

Thanks first of all to Michael Mirolla for showing faith in this book, and to the whole Guernica team—Connie McParland, Anna Van Valkenburg, and the rest—for their help with its publication and publicizing. My great luck with book covers continues, as I was fortunate to have David Moratto design and do the art for this cover; as you can see, the results are spectacular. My deepest gratitude to the Cecil Street workshop—first for agreeing to critique the stories despite the fact they weren't science fiction or fantasy tales, and second for their invaluable feedback. The comments I get from the Cecil Streeters always make my stories better. A special tip of the writerly and academic cap to Anneli Pekkonen for her never-flagging support. Above all, love and thanks to my family: my mother Freda, my late father Thomas, my sister Barbara (who is not *Sheila*), and my brother Ed.

About the Author

Allan Weiss lives in Toronto and teaches at York University as an Associate Professor of English and Humanities. He has published about two dozen short stories, both mainstream and fantasy/science fiction, in various journals and anthologies. His story cycle *Living Room* (Boheme Press) appeared in 2001, and another, *Making the Rounds*, was published in 2016 by Edge. Among his scholarly publications are articles on various topics in Canadian fiction, including the short story and Canadian science fiction and fantasy, and *A Comprehensive Bibliography of English-Canadian Short Stories, 1950–1983* (1988). He is Chair of the biennial Academic Conference on Canadian Science Fiction and Fantasy, and has edited three volumes of proceedings from the conference, most recently *The Canadian Fantastic in Focus*, which was published by McFarland in 2014.